THAIWATCH

F.A. Rawe

ISBN: 0615625347
ISBN-13: 978-0615625348

Dedication

To my family

October 1965

"That plane's gonna slam into the mesa!" Stony McGraw yelled over the roar as an old DC-3 barely cleared the treetops above them.

They watched as the plane began to slowly climb and managed to narrowly clear the edge of the mesa, only a couple of miles north of their hunting camp.

"They're gonna need some help. Let's go."

"I didn't hear any crash, Stony. In fact, the engines sounded just fine to me. Hell, they probably cleared the mesa and are twenty miles from here by now," Jim, his hunting partner answered.

It was sundown; the air was already getting crisp. It was going to be a cold night. Stony and Jim were bedding down the horses and setting up a simple night camp, taking advantage of the last light of day when they had heard the plane, low and slow. They were about 8,000 feet up in the southwest mountains of Colorado and the mesa probably topped out about 10,000 feet. It would be much colder up there, especially with the winds that always blew across those flattops.

Stony disagreed with his partner. "Somebody at least ought to check on them. If they did manage to set it down up there, or crashed and lived, they could die from exposure tonight. I'm going to check it out. If anything goes wrong, you can ride over in the morning." He started to unhitch the stock trailer from the Dodge 4x4.

"Alright, but at least grab some grub first," said Jim as he finished hobbling his horse.

"Don't have time. I'll just take a canteen and some jerky, we're losing daylight." He strapped on his pistol, a 38 caliber Smith and Wesson, just in case he ran into any varmints, but left his rifle in camp. It would be tough enough climbing without additional encumbrances. He stuffed a first-aid packet into a jacket pocket.

Stony worked his way in the old Dodge out to a narrow gravel road while trying to find a fire lane they had spotted earlier that ran along the bottom of the mesa. They had been on horseback at the time and hadn't given it much thought. By dead reckoning and hunches he managed to get to the bottom of the mesa with some light to spare, having driven as fast as he dared on the primitive trails. He stopped and dropped the shifter into 4-wheel low as the old pickup slowly crawled over fallen limbs and rocks up the ever steepening slope. He wanted the truck as close as possible in case of casualties. Finally, as the loose gravel and angle of the slope prevented any further progress, he stopped, slung the canteen over his shoulder and headed uphill on foot.

Moving upward wasn't easy. The slope was steep, covered with loose red rocks and unstable boulders that had fallen from up top over time and dotted with occasional shrubs. The last thirty feet or so was almost sheer cliff, but with enough rock holds to make the ascent possible.

He was about to clear the top, almost out of breath, when he noticed something strange. Silhouetted against the twilight was the plane, and nearby helicopter, idling. They weren't over a hundred yards away, up against the western edge of the mesa. The noise of the chopper drowned out the sounds of the men transferring boxes to it from the plane.

Instinctive caution made Stony decide to work his way around the side of the flattop and get a little closer look before making his presence known. The plane had obviously landed with no trouble. Stony was almost under the tip of the left wing when he slipped and fell about twenty feet into a crevasse. He wasn't seriously injured, just bruised up some and he had lost the canteen, but as he was climbing back up he saw, against the twilight sky, a long gun barrel easing over the edge just above him. They must have heard him scattering rocks as he fell. A head peered cautiously over the edge just a few feet above him. The guy spotted him and moved the butt to his shoulder, about to fire when Stony lunged upward, grabbed a handful of hair, slamming the face into the rock. Scrambling, he lifted the head with both hands and slammed it down again, hard. Then he pulled the body over the edge and let it drop below him, grabbing the long barrel as it went by. He felt he had no choice for what he had done. He couldn't take any chances, these guys were obviously smuggling something and they weren't likely to tolerate witnesses.

Luckily, the barrel he had grabbed turned out to be an American 12 gauge pump shotgun. The thought flicked by that if it had been something foreign, he might not have had time to figure it out. He eased around to the south, hoping to use the tail of the plane as cover if he had to move up top.

"That chopper's engine noise ain't helping any," he thought as he tried to figure out where the other two men were. He didn't care what they were smuggling, he just didn't want to die for it. Nothing to do but hunker down and wait for their move. It was a short wait. A round glanced off a rock just beside his head. Bits of gravel hit his face. A shadow moved to his right. No time to aim, he whirled with the shotgun and fired, slammed another shell home and fired again. The shadow joined his friend below. Stony warily peered over the top. Someone was running toward the chopper. Hoping his three count was right; he sprang over the top and skidded to a stop just behind the tail of the plane. His man wasn't over fifty feet away. He turned and fired a round at Stony, who then stepped into the open and fired. The runner stumbled; he was almost into the idling chopper. Stony pumped and fired again, then again. The runner was down. Stony pumped again but the Browning was empty. He pulled his 38 as he approached the body.

"Three up, three down. Now what do I do?" He was holstering his pistol when the sky lit up like daylight from three directions. A loudspeaker thundered from above, "FEDERAL AGENTS, THROW DOWN YOUR WEAPONS AND PUT YOUR HANDS IN THE AIR."

Stony complied. Three choppers with spotlights hovered above him. The noise of the idling chopper on the ground had masked their approach. One chopper broke off and sat down about a hundred feet to the north. The loudspeaker boomed again, repeating the message. With his hands still in the air, Stony motioned to the bloody body of the runner sprawled at his feet. Two men with weapons drawn approached. Hands high, Stony yelled above the din,

"You're too late. They're all dead. I'm the only one left and I'm not one of them."

Two more men appeared, one covered Stony, the others checked out the chopper and the plane.

"You do this?"

"No choice," answered Stony, "There's two more over the edge."

One of the men spoke into a radio and the choppers sat down around them. Stony told his story. He had only intended to offer assistance, but by the time he realized what was going on, it was too late. Things got out of hand and it became a matter of self defense.

They had seen his campfire. Eventually, they were satisfied. He checked out.

"Now your turn. What the hell is this all about?" he asked.

"Narcotics. We're DEA and this looks like a multi-million dollar haul."

A man approached. "Jeff, don't think we can get this chopper out tonight, it's been shot up a bit. We can leave a guard and take it out in the morning."

"Sounds good. I'm going to let McGraw here go. We can always get a statement in the future. We've got all we need for now," Jeff answered.

The man put out his hand, "Richard Ireland, CIA."

"I thought Jeff said you guys were DEA," countered Stony.

"We are. He's not."

"Just along for the ride. These guys were funding a terrorist group in Central America with drug sales in the U.S. I'm working the terrorist side of the case. By the way, I like the way you evidently operate under fire. Ever think of intelligence work? We could use a good man from time to time," said Richard.

"Sorry, I'm just a cattleman from eastern Colorado, over here for my annual hunting trip. Right now I'm just concerned with getting back to my camp in the dark," answered Stony.

"That pickup we saw down there yours?"

"It is."

"How about we chopper you back to your camp and you can get your vehicle at first light?"

"Sounds good to me." So after another hiring pitch from Richard, they set him down in a clearing a couple of hundred yards from his camp.

"Hello the camp," he yelled as he approached.

"Hello yourself," countered Jim as he came forward with a flashlight, "what the hell have you got yourself into this time?"

"It's a long story that I'll trade you for a cup of coffee, if there's any to be had." He put his arm over Jim's shoulder as they made their way through the trees and leaned close, "I've just been given a strange job offer. Would you be willing to look after my ranch if I were to be gone once in a while?"

CHAPTER 1

January 1968

"Sir, your wife is dead. Sir, please wake up!" The figure in the blood-stained white smock loomed over him, hand on his shoulder, "I'm sorry, sir. Your wife just passed away moments ago. We did everything we could; she was just too badly injured."

Stony McGraw sat bolt upright. He was shaking and sweating profusely. He ran his hands over his face, then roughly through his hair. The discordant hum of the window air conditioner brought him back to reality. He was no longer outside the emergency room of the local American military hospital where his wife had died, but in the upstairs bedroom of his Bangkok, Thailand home, the only air-conditioned room in the house.

"What the hell is going on? Why can't I shake this nightmare? She's been dead for a year now and I'm still reliving that day. I'm doing the best I can."

Sitting up on the side of the bed, his feet on the cool, bare, teakwood floor, elbows on his knees, he cradled his head in his hands for a few moments. He had to admit to being terribly disappointed with himself, frustrated by all the dead-end leads and well aware of the growing resentfulness, even bitterness surfacing within his personality. He raised his head and shook it, as if he could shake these feelings loose.

He glanced at the bedside clock. 5 AM. Although groggy, he knew there was no sense trying to get anymore sleep. Might as well shower and go out for some breakfast. He ate so seldom at home anymore the kitchen had become the province of the maid. Another trip to the Imperial. The Imperial hotel had a 24-hour coffee shop. He liked the Imperial and ate there often. It was close to the embassy; it had a good quiet restaurant for a relaxing meal and the coffee shop was clean. He had eaten there at all hours and the help knew him.

After a quick shower, Stony stepped out into the damp pre-dawn air. Six foot tall, 185 pounds, brown hair, deep blue eyes, with an almost muscular build, he could pass for an athlete in training, which he had never been. He moved easily, like a man whose body is used to muscular coordination, a man accustomed to hard work.

He was dressed in the acceptable embassy office attire of loose slacks, short sleeve dress shirt and tie, to which Stony added his own variation of pointy-toe, slope-heel leather cowboy boots. Nothing fancy, but the left one always held a small caliber pistol in a special holster. His shirts were flat tailed so he could wear them outside when he needed to. They and the pleated slacks easily hid his inside-the-belt holstered Smith & Wesson model 12 Airweight, 38 caliber revolver with its two inch barrel. Its 18 ounce weight made it easy to carry there.

He glanced around the carport and gave the car a quick security check in the limited early light. As he walked over to unlock the driveway gate, he inhaled deeply of the cool air that would shortly give way to the stifling heat of the coming tropical day. Newcomers would call it oppressively humid, but after eighteen months of acclimation it was reasonably pleasant to him. January was toward the end of the cool season in Bangkok, if you could call any season here cool. It wasn't quite as hot and humid the rest of the year and it didn't rain *every* day. All in all, January was probably one of the most pleasant months of the year. But it had rained briefly last night, giving the early morning air a clean feeling with a hint of the perfume of tropical flowers. The fragrance caused him to glance absently toward the back fence, across which the landlord cultivated prize-winning, aromatic, Thai Orchids as a hobby. They were hanging on wooden frames all over his small yard.

As he turned right off Soi 53 onto Sukhumvit Road, the main thoroughfare from his neighborhood to the center of town, he was pleased to see the traffic was light. Later it would be a teeming nightmare on this shop-lined boulevard, but at this pre-dawn hour it was quiet with the corrugated metal shutters of the side by side shops locked down tight. Reflections of streetlights glistened from the newly wet pavement. Within ten minutes Stony had crossed the railroad tracks, turned left a block before Vittayu-Wireless Road on which the American Embassy was located, and proceeded a block or so down a narrow street called Ruam Rhudi, into the small parking lot of the Imperial Hotel.

Stony slid into a booth in the brightly lit coffee shop and waived to the cook, nodding a yes to the unasked question on the cook's face. The cook went to work on Stony's usual breakfast. One of the two waiters was wiping a table and the other was leaning across the end of the counter, sleeping. He glanced toward the hotel pool just in time to see a beautiful insomniac as she bounced from the diving board into the water. The overhead fans stirred the air, the coffee was fresh and strong, he was halfway through his hamburger-steak and eggs, and deep into the English language Paris edition of the Herald-Tribune when he heard a familiar voice.

"You there in the cowboy boots."

"You look pretty used up, JJ," replied Stony.

"Used up is the word," JJ answered, "got a lead on a case and spent the whole fruitless night following it up." He called for coffee. At six foot three and 235 pounds, JJ was a rock solid 35 year old who had gone to college on a football scholarship. He still had the look of a linebacker, except for the thinning, early gray hair, which he kept closely cropped. That and his heavy, prominent chin, gave him the look of a bar bouncer you wouldn't want to tangle with. He was a rock-solid friend too. JJ's family had moved back to the states, for their own reasons, so he also lived alone for the moment.

"Official business?" Stony suspected not, for JJ, like the others was trying to help.

"Sort of. It will be when it's all put together. I'm getting closer. I can feel it."

"Just be careful. You know how Allan is about off assignment stuff," cautioned Stony, as he finished his toast.

"I'm not worried about the C-Y-A bureaucrat. I haven't slept since yesterday morning and I'm going home for a little shut-eye, as you would put it," complained JJ. Stony knew Allan would hit the roof.

"You know the rules JJ, if you're not on assignment, you keep office hours. Besides, we have a meeting at 9."

"Screw him. I'm beat." He took a long, last drink of his coffee.

"He'll start tracking you down." Stony thought for a moment. "How about taking a room here under another name. You can check in with me later."

"Done. Let's go."

Stony paid and proceeded to the embassy. Continuing down the same narrow street and turning just before Ruam Rhudi School, which his children had attended, he entered the embassy grounds through the back gate, around the PX gas station and over the short bridge that led to the parking lot. For security purposes, the embassy was surrounded by a wide moat-like canal. The only entry was by bridges at the front and back gates which were guarded by local Thai police.

Due to the great population of snakes in Thailand, the embassy used a small flock of geese, a dozen or so, to patrol the closely cropped grass and the parking lots. He noticed them dozing under a tree. The many stately trees and the manicured lawns gave the several acre sized grounds the look and feel of a classy estate. An old man was casting a wide fishnet into the canal, probably a gardener after an early morning meal. The natural balance of Thailand never ceased to amaze Stony. With mango, papaya, and banana trees everywhere, and plenty of fish in the ubiquitous canals, he doubted anyone ever went hungry here.

He parked under a tree that would shade his car from the brutal afternoon sun and ambled towards the 3-story gray monolith that housed the embassy and consulate offices. He glanced up at a chopper landing on the helipad atop the building. Since he had just finished a real breakfast, he didn't head for the cafeteria for his usual coffee and roll.

It was still before regular office hours, so Stony signed in with the Marine Security Guard. He was fond of the Marine

Guards; their home was sort of a second one for him. The TGIF parties at the Marine House were a great way to end a lonely week and sometimes he spent an enjoyable Saturday afternoon around their pool, whiling away the time with good beer and good conversation, and of course, watching the embassy secretaries cavorting in the water. It may have been somewhat insular, but sometimes a guy just wanted to hang around with other Americans.

After a little conversation, he climbed the stairs to the third floor office. He was still going over reports when the Chief of Station, Allan Huehner, strolled in, promptly at eight, cigarette in hand. A short, bald, overweight, out of shape, late forties chain smoker, he was a thoroughly pompous, obnoxious bureaucrat. His fingers and teeth were tobacco stained and because he perspired so much, he always had an unkempt, rumpled look about him.

"JJ's late again, isn't he? You'd better talk to him before I have to. I'm sick and tired of his unprofessional attitude. Oh yes, and don't you go away, you and I have that meeting at 9 sharp," said Allan as he lit another cigarette off the one in his hand.

"Who's this meeting with, Allan?"

"You'll see. JJ was supposed to join us, but you can handle it."

Stony could see it coming. Ever since his wife's death, Allan had been using job overload in his effort to pressure Stony to give up and go home. He had said it was for his own good, so the kids wouldn't lose their father too. There was a valid point to that, but Stony had promised his wife he would find her killers, and despite the mounting frustrations, he fully intended to do just that.

"I want you to meet your next assignment," said Allan as they made their way down the second floor hallway toward the Ambassador's office. Stony was already in a lousy mood, sick to death of this job overload bullshit.

The Ambassador's secretary, a competent, matronly older woman, announced them and led them into the inner office. Seated around a large, square, wooden coffee table on right angled couches were four people. The Ambassador, who rose to greet them, to his left was an older, short, heavy-set man with curly, receding hair, wearing an expensive, light gray, pin-striped suit, on the other couch sat an earnest looking, dark haired, thin younger man, similarly dressed, and to his left, a stunning, well-endowed, blue-eyed blond in a rather plain white blouse over a very short, white, mini-skirt, exposing an outstanding pair of well tanned legs, no nylons.

They were introduced and shook hands all around. The blond was beaming as she shook Stony's hand and held it a little too tight, and too long. Stony was uncomfortably conscious that the others were amused by this. Stern-faced he turned to them and they regained composure, averting his gaze.

"Well, Mister Ambassador," offered Allan, "how about informing Mister McGraw here of the plan?"

"Very well," answered the Ambassador. "Mister DePue," he cleared his throat, "Mister William Cullen DePue, is a personal representative of our president and he has arrived here, with his staff," he gestured towards the younger two, "on the final leg of a very high level, very sensitive mission. He has been authorized to offer the leader of Cambodia, Prince Sihanouk, a treaty of friendship and protection, together with an enormous amount of money, to be delivered in the future." He looked quizzically at Stony.

"Why, you may ask? Because we need his government's acquiescence for a small invasion into his northern provinces." He waived a hand toward the younger man, "I will let Mister Roger Stevens explain."

The younger man smiled with an air of tired superiority behind his horn-rimmed glasses, and then stood up.

"For many years now, the Prince has been playing the major powers against each other in his attempt to maintain overt neutrality, while at the same time allowing certain powers to pursue their own goals within his borders. Presently, this little game has been against the interests of the United States."

Stony had been studying the Southeast Asia situation in detail for a long time and wasn't in the mood for a course in 'Cambodian Diplomacy 101.'

"How about let's cut to the chase, Stevens."

The interruption seemed to temporarily unnerve the over-educated pipsqueak. Everyone frowned at Stony except the blond, who smiled. Stevens lowered his head so he could look at Stony over his heavy glasses,

"That is precisely what I am doing, Mister McGraw, if you will just be patient."

He looked around at the others with an air of pained tolerance and continued, "As I was saying. The President has sent our little group on this very hush-hush diplomatic sojourn to effect a concession towards our war effort. The enemy is enjoying somewhat of a safe haven status in eastern Cambodia. We wish to invade the area but in order to do this; we must secure permission, or at least the tacit non-interference, from the Cambodian government. Therefore, we have arranged a meeting with certain high government officials for tomorrow evening in Phnom Penh."

Stony was already in a bad mood and was becoming disgusted. He had gotten the picture a long time ago. "Tell you what, Stevens, why don't you just let me know what the hell I am doing here, then I can be on my way and you can continue with your long winded explanation."

"Well, in that particular matter, I'm not quite sure. I…"

The Ambassador interrupted. He stood up and said rather sternly, "Mister McGraw, you have been assigned by your office to bodyguard this delegation. Transportation leaves for the airport at thirteen hundred hours. If you would care to make preparations…" He waived his hand toward the door.

Great. Now he had hacked off the Ambassador. He realized none of these people had anything to do with his problems. As he was about to apologize, he happened to glance at the blond, who smiled and partially opened her legs, revealing the crotch of her lacy white panties. Whether anyone saw it, he didn't know; they seemed to be staring intently at him. What he did know was that he didn't like women like her, smug and aggressive, thinking every man would die to get into those panties. He looked hard into her still smiling eyes and stood, "I'll be there. Now if you'll excuse me."

He wasn't twenty feet down the hallway when he heard the tap of high heels behind him on the terrazzo floor.

"Stony…"

He continued walking.

"Mister McGraw!"

He stopped and turned toward her, "What do you want?"

17

"I'm sorry, but we seem to have gotten off to a bad start. I didn't realize my little flirting would offend you."

He wasn't sympathetic. She was probably looking for an excuse to get out of there herself. Maybe she expected this little encounter to lead to something. He had other ideas.

"Flirting is a hellava lot more subtle, lady. And I'm not offended. This is Bangkok and easy women are as common as flies on cowshit."

"Lady? I do have a name, you know."

"I'm sure you do. I must have forgotten it already, what was it again?"

She pursed her lips in what Stony interpreted as feigned offense, "It's Vera Legette. I am the administrative assistant for this mission."

"Well, Miss Legette, I will see you at one o'clock." He turned and continued toward his office. He didn't hear her walking away, figured she was still glaring at him. He smiled as the thought crossed his mind that maybe he should wiggle his ass for the bitch. Years ago he would have enjoyed all that as a playful encounter, but now he couldn't help but reflect on what a bitter person he had become lately.

He was cleaning his 38 and a sawed-off shotgun when Allan returned.

"You should have been more courteous to them, Stony. They're real live VIP's, traveling on Air Force 2." He lit a cigarette.

"Probably should have been, but I wasn't. Those kind are way too impressed with themselves and I tend not to feed their egos. If this little scheme works, the pompous fat guy will be hailed as a great diplomat and his little team will bask in diplomatic glory, when all they are doing is buying some petty politicians. How hard is that? As for me, I hope I can make it for two days without punching that condescending kid out."

"Well, cheer up, Stony. That blonde's obviously got the hots for you. I'll guarantee you'll be banging her before the trip's over. Damn, I envy you, she's sexier'n hell."

Stony put down his pistol and stood up.

"Let me tell you something, Mister. Any decent looking woman with a genuine sweet personality can easily overcome a certain lack of physical beauty, but the most beautiful, most desirable woman in the world... if she's a bitch, she's just a bitch."

Allan stared at him for a long moment, "My, my, what a bitter man you have become."

"I just don't like her kind."

Stony was visiting with the Marine Security Guard in the entrance lobby of the embassy when his trio came out of the elevator. He turned and nodded. The fat man nodded in return, but no one smiled. Stony picked up his brown canvas duffel bag containing the shotgun, among other things, and followed them through the front doors. The Ambassador had made his limousine and driver available. The driver opened the rear door. The blond and the kid got in. Stony started toward the right front door, but DePue touched his arm and indicated he should join them in the back.

"Mister McGraw, please. There is plenty of room."

He joined them. As soon as they were underway, DePue addressed the group.

"I may be in charge of this diplomatic mission, but Mister McGraw is now in charge of security. I would appreciate it if you would give him your utmost cooperation. This could be a very dangerous undertaking, as has been explained to each of you previously, and I am very serious when I add that your very life may depend on Mister McGraw here." He turned to Stony.

"And, Mister McGraw, I must add, this has been a long, tiring journey for us so I ask that you be tolerant of our little idiosyncrasies."

Stony grinned, "In other words, lighten up. Fair enough. I've got a lot on my mind right now, but none of it has to do with you. Maybe we could start fresh," he put out his hand, "They call me Stony."

"They call me Mister DePue," as he shook Stony's hand. This elicited a smile from the blond, "and they call me Vera."

Everyone looked at the stern faced, earnest young man.

"Oh, all right." He grudgingly extended his hand, "I'm Roger."

"Well, that's better." Stony turned to the old man and grinned, "No offense sir, but if I had a name like DePue, I'd just as soon be called William."

All three grinned and the atmosphere lightened noticeably. Still, the rest of the ride to the airport was in silence.

Their plane was parked off on a side runway, surrounded by an American Military Police contingent. They boarded 'Air Force 2', obviously a VIP aircraft, beautifully appointed. To say it was plush would be an understatement. They boarded via the forward door, which opened into a section of first class passenger seats, about twenty or so. DePue led the way through these into the next section, a lounge with plush white chairs and couches, a wet bar, a large conference table, lots of electronics and lushly carpeted in the presidential blue.

Turning to Stony, he said, "The bathrooms are through that door, between this section and the bedrooms. Would anyone care for a drink?"

The blond, Vera, began making a Manhattan for herself. She looked inquiringly at DePue, who shrugged his shoulders, "I believe I will, my dear. Thank you."

Stony kind of figured from his actions that DePue sort of hoped his position of importance might get him somewhere with the blond, but though she was cordial, she remained somewhat distant. Stony asked if there was any beer and she handed him one, in a bottle, of course.

The young man addressed Stony, "If you will permit me, Mister, ah, Stony, I could provide some information on our destination."

Stony has spent a couple of hours this morning studying what he had on Cambodia and the layout of its capital, but in the interest of amiability, he agreed, since the young man, Roger, seemed to downright enjoy demonstrating his knowledge of things.

"Well, Phnom Penh, the capital, sits at the confluence of three rivers, the Tonle Sap, the Mekong, and the Bassac. It is a beautiful city of some six hundred thousand people. There is much evidence still remaining of the French colonial influence. The city takes its name from a beautiful temple called Wat Phnom. It and the royal palace are in the center of the city, as is a magnificent Catholic cathedral. By the way, they do not call themselves Cambodians, but Khmers. This is also the name of the language they speak, and French, not English is their second language. Also, they call their country Kampuchea. Cambodia is merely the English version of that. Otherwise, the country is much like the rest of Southeast Asia, except for its noticeable lack of industrialization. We will be staying at one of the royal residences, but I do not know which one. I only wish we could find the opportunity to visit Angkor Wat, but it is far to the northeast of Phnom Penh and besides the lack of time, security could be a problem. It is the ancient capital of Cambodia, with some magnificent temples, but after its capture by the Thais in the fourteen hundreds, it was abandoned. It is still one of the greatest archeological sites in Southeast Asia."

Stony listened attentively, thanked him when he finished and settled back to enjoy the view, and another beer.

The flight was short, just over half an hour, accompanied by the brutal dive-in landing common these days to Southeast Asia. They were met at the airport by a military convoy of four jeeps and two olive-drab sedans, one for them and one for their welcoming delegation. The greeting was formal, not all that friendly, and Stony had no idea who the officials were or how they ranked. They were whisked away at a good clip through the dusty, crowded streets and out towards the other side of the city to a seedy palace on the outskirts.

The large palace compound was walled-in with local police patrolling the outside perimeter and a squad of militia inside. The large main building was off-white stucco, with a red tiled roof, U-shaped, three floors with wide verandahs surrounding the bedroom areas. There were no glass windows, just louvered shutters outside screens. No air-conditioning, but the verandahs and ceiling fans provided a reasonable cooling effect. Their escort directed them and the baggage carriers to the third floor and informed them that there were four rooms provided, three with adjoining baths and one without. The rooms were connected by doors that could be locked from either side.

"Well, in that case, we must decide who must share a bath," declared Roger.

"I've already decided that," said Stony. "The woman obviously requires a private bath; I will take the adjoining room for security purposes, which places me square in the middle of everyone. I guess you guys will have to do the sharing."

The young man looked questioningly at DePue, who merely nodded and strolled in the direction of his room. After a few steps, he turned, glanced at his watch, "According to a cable I received in Bangkok, our 'Chargé d' affaires ad interim' has invited us to dinner and will be picking us up within the hour. I suggest you use the available time to freshen up."

"Chargé d' affaires?" asked Roger, "Don't we have an ambassador here?"

"Called home for consultation, Roger. Any further questions?"

Roger nodded negatively and followed DePue towards their rooms. Stony checked out his room, ran a wet washcloth over his face, threw on some 'stink-purty', hid the shotgun temporarily inside the shower curtain, and stepped outside to view the surroundings. He noticed the shutter screens didn't lock, although the doors did, that a heavy vine climbed from the ground to the top of the building, not good, that the wooden railings were none too secure, and that the blonde was leaning against her door frame watching him.

"Would you care to examine my room?"

"Matter of fact, I would," Stony said as he stepped past her. It was the same as his, large, about twenty feet square, an adjoining musty-smelling bath, single ceiling fan, the door flanked on either side by wide louvered screen windows. It was also furnished exactly like his, with a simple double bed, large teak wardrobe, and a dressing table and chair. In the middle of the east wall was a doorway that led to his own room. He walked over and slid the bolt latch closed.

"I appreciate your concern for my safety, Stony, but that was the one door I intended to leave unlocked. In case you need to rush in and save me, of course." She walked out and headed towards Stony's room, "Just to see what it looks like."

Stony stepped out onto the verandah to continue checking the area. Their four rooms constituted the entire third floor west wing of the building, facing north, with the blonde's room on the far west end.

The dinner was at the Ambassador's residence, catered by his staff, even though he was in the States "for consultation." That was a diplomatic term meaning the two countries weren't getting along right now.

The dinner was enjoyable and when the diplomatic types adjourned to discuss hot foreign affairs topics, Stony instead, accepted an offer of a glass of brandy and a cigar. Stepping out into the still warm tropic night air, he spotted a table and chairs and made himself comfortable. Security wouldn't be a problem here. The cigar was mild yet full flavored and while he probably didn't have more than a couple a year, when he did, he enjoyed them. As he took a long pleasurable pull on the cigar, his thoughts were carried back home to Colorado.

He remembered another cigar custom that had developed over the years. He had a friend that started visiting about once a year, and they had developed a tradition that brought a smile to his face. The very first year, after a hard day of building fence, they decided to check the cattle herd in a nearby pasture. The friend, being a fun loving sort of fellow, threw a cooler of beer, some beef jerky and a pack of cigars into the bed of the pickup. They drove into the middle of the herd, set themselves up on the rails in the back of the truck and began to seriously evaluate each cow and calf. The conversation drifted, the empty cans began to accumulate around them, and the herd lost interest in the cowboys and drifted away. Around sunset, the jerky gone and the cigars smoked, Stony unsteadily pulled the last two beers out of the cooler.

The friend, old Steve, popped the top of his can,

"By gawd Stony, this is the life! It's been one of those really fine days, but I gotta tell ya, its beginning to come up a chill and I've got a helluva hunger building, what say we head on back and talk your sweet wife into throwing a couple steaks on the grill?"

"Way ahead of you, ol' buddy, I told her we'd probably get to the house around sundown. What I didn't know was the sorry shape we'd be in."

Even the rough ride across the prairie couldn't prevent old Steve from passing out before they reached the edge of the pasture, so Stony managed to handle the wire gate and drove home on the thankfully deserted back country roads. His wife wasn't too happy at their inebriated state, but she good naturedly served up a hearty steak and potato supper which his friend rallied to enjoy and even entertained them with his alcohol inspired uninhibited conversation. Although they had toned it down somewhat over the years, the cigars and beer herd inspection had become an annual tradition.

Damn, he wished he could get back home. He had never been so damned sick of a situation in his life. And now he was babysitting these clowns.

His solitude was interrupted by a shapely spike-heeled leg draped across the table in front of him. She was still wearing white. He stood up and started towards the door, "You know doll, white ain't your color."

"Then what would you suggest?"

"Red!"

On the return trip to their lodgings, in the dark back seat of the sedan, she twice ran her toes up his boots and onto his calves. Twice he pulled away. She sure did know how to get a guy, and although he hated to admit it, she was getting to him.

Upon arrival at their temporary dwellings, Stony made a thorough inspection of the area and in each of their rooms. They had been warned about opposing factions but he had noted the placement of the guards, both inside and outside the compound's walls. All seemed to be as well as could be expected, for the present, so he showered and hit the rack. He was a light sleeper and had decided to make security checks often during the night.

It wasn't long before he heard the connecting door to the blonde's room open. He had noticed the latch had been opened when he had returned from dinner. She had evidently done it when she 'checked out' the room earlier.

He lay still as she slid naked into his bed. He had fully expected this, and after the ride back to the rooms… She slipped her arm around him and he turned to face her, "You don't quit, do you?"

"Quitting is for losers."

26

CHAPTER 2

Her warm, soft body was rapidly awakening his long neglected libido. What the hell, he thought to himself; why not take advantage of this. He'd been dealt a pretty crappy hand lately, and besides, wasn't this every red-blooded guy's dream? He didn't really like the woman, but he had to admit, when it came to raw, unadulterated lust, she was a ten out of ten. By rapid stages his resistance totally disappeared. Long dormant passion was stimulated and raging animal lust was aroused in spades. She wanted him and she was going to get him and his year-long buildup of cravings.

He began kissing her gently, then more firmly, open mouthed, their tongues fought it out. She grabbed him, massaging his groin; the breathing was heavy and labored. So much for foreplay, he slid over onto her. To hell with a slow gentle beginning, she was already grinding, so he went at it more forcefully than he normally would. It felt so good. She began to moan, then to quiver, he played her well. She was gasping for breath. They were sweating more heavily now and working hard, grinding, thrusting, pounding and finally the pent up bursting of relief. They collapsed together.

He lay there awhile, but instead of being sated, he wanted more. His re-awakening hormones were raging, he wanted more than ordinary sex with this woman; he wanted to ravish her, to consume her, to spend his long built up passion. He grabbed a handful of sheet, reached down and wiped her dry. He slid down and began kissing her slim soft ankle, her solid delicious calves, up the inside of her well tanned thighs. He nibbled gently and then let his tongue do the work. With measured pressure and tongue thrusts, he brought her along slowly until her breathing quickened, then deepened. She was moaning as she exhaled, grabbing at his hair and sinking her fingernails into his scalp. Still, he continued as she quivered, she jolted, she begged him to stop, and finally, he did.

He sat up and looked at her. She was grinning up at him through her exhaustion. Damn, she was beautiful even in this dimly lit room, with her long blonde hair spread across the pillow, some of it wafting across her face.

"Come on, we'll clean up," he said as he pulled her up by the hand. She tried to stand but slumped; he grabbed her and carried her to the shower. She had a silly grin on her passion-weary face, and she giggled spontaneously, but she could stand, sort of. He cleaned them both up, dried her off and carried her back to the bed before returning to brush his teeth.

When he returned to the bed, she was sleeping. He lay beside her, pulled her over; put her head on his shoulder, his arm around her. They lay there awhile in that pleasurable after-sex swoon.

He must have dozed off, because he was awakened by a warm, wet, pleasant sensation. After enjoying it as long as he could, he pulled her up over him. He always lasted so much longer the second time around. They tried several positions and each time she climaxed, they tried another. He brought her off several times and finally ended up with her on bottom and him on top. Sweating profusely, their grinding stomachs were making squishing noises, which made her giggle, so he turned her over, put a pillow under her belly and continued thrusting until he had spent himself.

They were both exhausted now and holding each other close, fell into a deep restful sleep.

Something woke him. He wasn't sure what. It was still very dark outside, but he figured it must be near dawn. He listened carefully for any noise, breathing as quietly as he could. Nothing. A shadow moved on the verandah outside his window, towards DePue's room. Stony slowly eased his arm from around Vera and put his hand over her mouth, which as he expected, awakened her. He whispered, "Don't make a sound."

He quietly put on his slacks, stuck the 38 in his belt, grabbed the shotgun from under the edge of the mattress where he had put it before hitting the rack, and eased to the door. He slowly pulled it open and peered out. The shadow was a dozen feet to his right. It turned. Stony waited just a second, long enough to know he had been seen, then ducked back inside, leaving the door open. Cautiously, the shadow stepped inside the opened door, a machete held up in both hands. Stony waited. The shadow took one more step inside when Stony swung the shotgun swiftly across his ankles. He went down, falling hard, the machete sliding across the floor. Stony brought the butt of the shotgun down with all his might onto the attackers head, crushing the skull. He raced over and grabbed the machete, rushing back to one side of the door just in time for another dark figure to jump into the room. Holding the machete with both hands, Stony swung the blade straight across the figure's belly. With a blood-stifled cry, the figure doubled over and fell to the floor, the machete still imbedded into his stomach, which was copiously oozing blood and other things across the thin carpet. Two down. How many more? They were so quiet. Two dead and still hardly any noise. Not for long. Vera screamed and Stony turned to see another one in the door. Stony whirled, slammed the door into his face, yanked it back and kicked the intruder in the nuts. He doubled over and Stony punched him with an uppercut to the face, sending him reeling out onto the verandah, then grabbed the shotgun as the guerilla struggled to pull a pistol and Stony let go with two quick rounds of double-aught buckshot. The intruder hurled backwards through the railing and out into nothingness. Three down.

Stony almost joined them. As he glanced outside, up and down the verandah, the startled guard unit down on the ground fired several volleys at him. He grabbed the floor just in time. He heard a lot of shouting and firing and a few obvious victims screaming. When the firing stopped, he raced over and opened the door joining his and Roger's rooms. DePue had done the same thing and was standing in the next adjoining door in a bathrobe. Roger was in pajamas.

"Both of you. In here! Now!"

Vera, wide-eyed, was sitting up in bed, wrapped only in the sheet. So much for decorum.

"All of you, into my bathroom. Lock the door, get down and stay quiet. Not a word." Silence wasn't all that necessary now, but that way they wouldn't bother Vera and belabor the obvious. With only screens for windows and unless they were very sound sleepers, they had undoubtedly heard the earlier athletic events. It was sort of amusing to see these big shots so reduced by fear. The men had both paled and walked across the mattress on the way to the bathroom to avoid stepping near the bodies on the floor.

The first streaks of dawn began to appear and he could see around outside. Several soldiers were running towards their rooms, rifles at the ready. He turned and threw the shotgun onto the bed and slipped the pistol into the back of his belt. No sense drawing fire from over-zealous troops. Their sergeant stepped into the room and looked at Stony, who held up three fingers and drew them across his throat. The sergeant grinned, turned and said something to his men. They entered the room and dragged the bodies out onto the verandah. A couple of them gagged when it became obvious that the one near the door was almost cut in half. The sergeant gave Stony the thumbs up sign. Some of the palace staff soon showed up with buckets and rags and began to clean things up. Stony stepped over to the bathroom and pounded on the door.

"Alright. Everybody out." They unlocked the door and gingerly stepped into the room.

"Seems that last night I heard some fellow say they would pick us up for breakfast this morning. I've worked up a pretty good appetite and I need a shower. Best you folks do the same." He smiled at Vera, who smiled back.

"I…I don't know if I could face food right now," offered Roger.

"It will be alright, Roger," said Stony, "Have a shower and things might just look up after that. It's okay, things are safe now. Shut the door behind you."

As soon as the door was shut, Vera grabbed him, hugging him tightly for a few minutes. He returned her embrace. When she let go, she kissed his still naked chest, "Thanks, I really needed that just now." She pulled the sheet off her beautiful naked body, rolled it up into a ball and handed it to him. She kissed his lips and whispered, "I'd better get ready now."

He enjoyed watching that body disappear through the door. Funny how a little friendly sex can change a person's attitude. She seemed to be softening and he was actually beginning to like her.

They were picked up by a very agitated Chargé and escorted again to the sojourning ambassador's residence. DePue had regained his official composure and surprised Stony by telling the Chargé that while it had been a very frightening experience, Mister McGraw seemed to have it well in hand. They had a couple of hours before the meeting with the Cambodian officials, so while the rest of them went over plans and strategies, Stony found a couch in a nearby room and caught a short nap. He wondered how Vera was holding up with so little sleep.

"Hey cowboy." It was Vera, carrying a tray with two coffee cups and a carafe. "We're leaving in a few minutes, better have a cup and wake up."

He sat up and grinned, "A cup of wake up would come in mighty handy right now, ma'am."

They were convoyed under heavy guard to a government building and after preliminary formalities, the diplomats got down to their bargaining session. They talked all day and into the early evening. A meal was served in an adjoining room, during which they continued their talks. Messengers came and went. The talks careened from heated agitation to relaxed conviviality and back again. It was a long, boring afternoon for Stony. He watched as Vera, incredibly, never flagged. She was all business, taking notes, directing the embassy staff, and advising DePue and his assistant Roger Stevens. Finally, just before midnight, DePue and his Cambodian counterpart stood up shook hands and the respective groups departed.

"What next?" asked Stony.

Roger answered, "Another night in that horrible palace, I suppose. I won't be able to get a moment of sleep."

"Not so my young colleague," said DePue, "I am not interested in tempting fate again. We will be escorted to the airport and will spend the rest of the night safe in a Bangkok hotel. We will enjoy a good, safe night's sleep, as late as we please." He glanced at Vera, "Some of us must be very tired indeed."

In the sedan on the way to the airport, Stony was curious about how things went, so he asked, "Did you folks get what you wanted back there?"

"Not yet. It will take more negotiations," answered DePue.

"They kept raising one technical issue after another," added Roger, "I just don't understand it; most of those issues just didn't matter."

"Roger, my boy, experience will answer your questions," instructed DePue, "you see, I have learned over the years that when third world countries deal with the United States, no matter what they say, what they all want is all the same – more money."

"Then damnit, why didn't they just…"

"Of all the lessons I could give you about tonight, young man, I will select only one: If you admit to the game, you lose the game."

"Roger, you might could use some lessons from an ol' country boy," said Stony.

"Like what, for instance."

"Like whittlin', for instance."

Roger was obviously getting very perturbed at this new turn in the conversation, "What the hell has whittling got to do with the subject we are presently discussing?" It seemed everyone but Roger was amused.

"Let me tell you a story, Roger. A few years ago I found an ol' boy who wanted to sell a grain drill that I needed. Now a grain drill is a piece of agricultural equipment used for planting seed. Anyway, I went to see him but his price was half again what I could pay. So I picked up a stick and began whittling on it with my pocket knife. Now that right there is a country message that means we need to get to haggling. I asked if he'd gotten any rain lately, then we discussed the price of calves and half a dozen other subjects. Every once in a while, we'd even talk a little about the grain drill. After about an hour of whittling, he lowered his price and I upped my offer. We came to an agreement and we both got what we wanted."

"And just what is the point of all this, may I ask?"

"Roger, I figure you must be a smart cookie to be in the position you are in but you ain't got the common sense of a fence post. Whittlin' is just slow moving haggling. Those boys back there today were just whittlin'. They probably didn't give a damn about any of those objections they raised. Whatever amount of money Uncle Sam was offering, they were trying for more."

"Very perceptive, Mister, er, Stony, very perceptive."

"Well I don't know a lot about diplomacy, but if I were you, I'd do a little bombing, to make it look like you've lost patience, then come back to the table with a low offer. I'll bet they would be a might more receptive next time."

34

They re-boarded the plane without incident and landed in Bangkok just after 2:00 AM. The pilot had radioed ahead and the ambassador's limo was waiting on the tarmac when they came to a stop. The driver dropped Stony off at the embassy before escorting the little group to the ambassador's guest house. They wouldn't have to stay in a hotel after all. Stony had said good-bye to them and even kissed the lady's hand.

After a short night's sleep he was in the office just before seven, writing up his report and enjoying the relatively clean air before chain smoking Allan polluted it, which promptly at the hour he did.

He poured himself a cup of coffee, "Well, well what do you know. Smile if you got any."

"Cram it, Allan. We got back here after two this morning. I'm not in the mood for any crap from a bureaucrat. I was going to sleep in, guess I should have."

"Oh relax, Stony. It's a good thing you are here. I, that is we, have a very important meeting this morning."

"And just who the hell is *this* meeting with?"

"The Ambassador, the Defense Attaché, JJ supposedly, you and me," answered Allan, "and JJ's late again. I'm not going to stand for this much longer. I intend to make a memo for record of this and include it in his annual evaluation. He simply can't get away with this unprofessional behavior. I am in charge of this office and he is going to learn that or else."

Stony thought to himself, "Give a bureaucrat a little power…" He turned to Allan, "Got any idea what this meeting is all about?"

"Listen to this; it'll give you a clue."

"Now what?" asked Stony as he caught an audio tape Allan pitched to him.

Stony listened. It was a speech by President Johnson in which he said, among other things, that the "United States has no assassination squads stationed in the Republic of South Vietnam." Stony was amused that in his Texas drawl Johnson always pronounced Vietnam as if it rhymed with ham. The speech was so old; Stony had heard it in the original on Armed Forces radio.

Once again he regretted taking this assignment. Always before, he had been recruited for one-shot deals. He was a filler, a "freelancer" as Richard his agency monitor, had put it. This "tour of duty" assignment was frustrating, putting in time and taking on whatever came up. If the ranch back in Colorado hadn't been in such a financial mess he would never had done it. He was desperately squeezed for time as it was, trying to find his wife's killers while working on a ridiculous scheme, dreamed up in Washington, to bring remnants of the old Chinese Nationalist forces, still living in the mountains of northern Southeast Asia into the Vietnam War as diversionary forces. It sounded good on paper, but as he ruminated about it, he had his doubts.

Back in 1949 when the Chinese Nationalists, called the Kounintang, lost the civil war to Mao Tse Tung's Communists on mainland China, the Nationalist leader, Chiang Kai-Shek moved everything and everyone he could to a large island off the southeast coast named Taiwan, at that time called Formosa. However, a large Nationalist army contingent was trapped up against Southeast Asia in southwest China. Rather than surrender, they decided to melt into the mountains and jungles and have since been operating on their own as local warlords engaged in trade and smuggling. They pretty much ignore the national boundaries of Burma, Thailand, Laos and sometimes even North Vietnam. The United States for many years has aided their survival with financial assistance and they, in turn provided much needed intelligence information. So, even before this "harebrained scheme" as Stony referred to it was concocted, we had a good working relationship with them. Now, McNamara and his Pentagon whiz-kids had dreamed up a plot to tie up North Vietnam's leaders with a two-front war by having the Chinats feign a high-tech, phony, large-scale attack on their northwestern border. The negotiations had proceeded to the point of a tentative agreement, subject to proper payment by the U.S. Under orders, Stony had worked out a payment drop of five million dollars to be delivered Friday night. Personally, he didn't believe the scheme had a snowball's chance, but he would do his job as he had agreed to do. If they had asked his opinion, he would have mentioned that it had been almost twenty years since these men had been in regular forces, that they were lightly armed compared with the North Viet army, that they would probably clash as much with the H'mong tribesman, already trained by the CIA to counter Laotian communists, as with the North Viets, that he doubted they had either the numbers or the will to actually put up much of a fight, that they did not have sophistication to properly operate McNamara's electronic gadgets, and lastly, he believed they were just playing the role until they got their money.

Thinking of which, "Is the Chinat payoff still on schedule?" he asked as he leaned into Allan's office.

"Money will be here Friday noon, delivery up north just like you planned for Friday night. I suggest you take JJ with you, just in case," answered Allan.

"JJ's pretty busy, why don't you come along?" Stony feigned sincerity. Allan just glared back.

The meeting was held in the Defense Attaché's "Secure Room." The Colonel was very proud of this room. The floor, walls and ceiling were covered with sound-deadening materials – all white for easier detection of any changes. It was actually a room suspended within a room, so that all sides could be easily checked for bugging devices. No phones, minimum electrical wiring and indirect cooling and air movement were provided. Only about 12 by 12 feet square, it was simply furnished with a table and six chairs and a wooden easel in one corner for charts and maps. In a bit of overkill, the outer room had motion sensors in two corners connected to an alarm, which of course, had to be turned off prior to each use. Absolutely no access was allowed unless personally escorted by the colonel or his aide, and it was used only for classified briefings.

The Ambassador was late, so Colonel White made small talk. The Colonel, full medalled, khaki clad, plopped his overweight frame into a chair and lit one of his ever present cigars. He glanced about for an ashtray. Allan slid his across the table midway between them. After politely inquiring about any progress in Stony's on-going investigation of his wife's murder, he drifted into gossip about the local social scene. Colonel White seldom missed a party. This was his swan-song assignment and there wasn't much else to do as far as he was concerned. The official cocktail parties of two hours duration merely warmed him up for the evening. Stony had seen him and his wife at the Derby Club often.

The Ambassador rushed in carrying a briefing paper he had probably just read. It really didn't tell him much anyway. It didn't matter; this was Colonel White's show. The Ambassador in reality was just being informed. He glanced disdainfully at the smokers. The thought crossed Stony's mind that he probably considered himself the perfect physical specimen for his age. He was a tall, well-dressed, go-getter type, often with a brusque, no-nonsense manner. A political appointee, former general officer, he was probably just what they needed in this post right now.

The colonel began. "I've just had the room swept, so we may speak freely." Using his best briefing manner the Colonel continued. "Gentlemen, the classification of this briefing is TOP SECRET. Now as you know, our Commander in Chief, President Johnson, in a speech not long ago disavowed the stationing of assassination personnel within the borders of South Vietnam. This was brought about by nothing less than the coercion of the Press and is another example of the media interfering with our war effort. Having made a public statement on the subject, the President's word must be kept. However, the problem remains. As you are probably aware, most of the assassinations there have been political and have occurred between the Vietnamese themselves. Our problem is, we believe, strictly military with strictly military consequences. Unfortunately, the political higher-ups don't agree. Therefore, an inter-agency solution has been tentatively worked out. The assassination team will be stationed here in Bangkok and flown to its mission."

Stony cleared his throat, "Question Colonel, who is the target? You haven't mentioned that, and what it has to do with our office?" He thought he knew.

"Good questions, Mr. McGraw. The target is, rather are, enemy agents with transmitters situated within the protection of pacified villages. They form an efficient intelligence gathering network hiding behind our appeasement policy which limits our ability to take appropriate action against them. If we initiate military action against the individual VC agent involved, that is interpreted as an assassination and every damned infantry squad in the country seems to have a reporter with them. As to your second question, your agency has kindly volunteered your office as the assassination team."

Stony shot a quick look at Allan, who studied the table top intently.

The Colonel continued. "Let me illustrate the concept we propose." He placed a map of Southeast Asia on the easel.

"At precisely 1900 hours on the day of the mission, our two man team will board a chopper on the helipad atop the embassy. They will then be transported to the airbase south of here at Sattahip. There they will board a small Air Force passenger jet for the roughly 45 minute flight to South Vietnam and will land at one of three U.S. military airbases, depending on the target area. There they will be met by a hand-picked team of Special Forces personnel and be choppered to a site near the intended target. The Special Forces unit will escort our team into the village, but can in no way participate in the specific mission. Our team will take out the operator or operators, there is usually only one, place all his equipment together and destroy it with a thermite grenade. A quiet but hasty departure should have all personnel out of the immediate area prior to the likely incineration of the hut. A flak jacket and jungle fatigues will be issued to our personnel by the Special Forces. Weapon is your choice. The course will be reversed and if our estimate is correct, the entire mission will take approximately six hours and our team will arrive back here at the embassy shortly after midnight to 0100 hours. There upon they will descend the stairs and sign out with the Marine Security Guard as if merely working late. I, of course, will require a debriefing session sometime the next work period. Any questions?"

Stony spoke, "Colonel White, you seem to have worked this all out with the precision of a military close-order drill. I hope you have also worked out contingency plans for the inevitable glitches that will occur. For instance, my weapon of choice is my 38 revolver, and I doubt a quiet departure will be possible after that. We can only hope the war has cowed the villagers into a 'see no evil' attitude. Also, it is my guess we will find the VC radio operator in a hole under his hut. Surprise will be our only recourse – hit him hard and burn him out. Your thermite grenade is a good idea. They can replace the operator quickly but the equipment will have to be carried down the Ho Chi Minh trail to replace local stocks. When do you plan the first mission?"

Allan grinned, "Tonight. You and JJ. We'll see if the Colonel's system works. Now if you have nothing further Colonel."

Back in the office, Allan turned quickly to Stony, "Just say a word, Stony, and I'll relieve you from duty and have your ticket home by noon tomorrow."

"I may have to extend my tour if you don't stop hindering my progress," answered Stony lightly, intending to defuse the tension.

"Fat chance. Besides, what progress? You've hit nothing but a stone wall so far. Just remember you have a job to do here and you're spending entirely too much time on something that should be left to criminal professionals. You know my feelings on this. I've tried my best to have you sent home but you've gone over my head and behind my back and now it's out of my hands. It sure would be a shame if those nice kids lost their dad too; after all they've gone through, just because he's consumed by vengeance."

"Justice, Allan, justice!" Stony was angry now. He leaned close to Allan, "I fully intend to find the killers and bring them to justice, one way or the other, despite your well-intentioned interference. And I'll tell you this. If you are the reason I don't find them, you will answer to me for that."

"Are you threatening me?" Allan tried to sound defiant as he backed away, his face betraying his fear.

"You're damn right!"

Allan backed towards his office, glaring. Stony left for lunch. It wouldn't do to flatten the boss.

The Chief of Station, Allan Huehner, an administrative type, was a company man all the way. JJ said he had an advanced degree in 'cover your ass.' This made it difficult for the Stony's and JJ's. They regarded themselves as street agents. They resented Allan's caution and interference and he, in turn, resented their lack of regard for his rules. He was a difficult person to get along with, a thorough bureaucrat, petty and authoritative. Never married as far as anyone knew. Maybe it was because of his despicable sense of humor. As JJ put it, "He doesn't consider a joke very good unless it ruins your lunch." He wasn't socially liked by the embassy staff either, having hit on almost every woman there.

THAIWATCH

The embassy had a new air-conditioned lunchroom now, but the food wasn't any better; they still put mashed potatoes in the lasagna, for instance. The former lunchroom had more charm, Stony thought, with its elevated construction to avoid snakes and high water, its tropic-worn wood, glassless screen windows with their drop down shutters, and ceiling fans turning slowly. It just felt right. This terrazzo and glass modern version with all the stainless steel was probably more sanitary, but it had no character. And the food. It really was our fault, he surmised, expecting Thai's to cook American and European dishes they'd never tasted in the original themselves.

There was one dish that could be relied upon anywhere in Asia. Whether it was called 'nasi goreng' in Indonesia, 'kow pot' in Thailand, or just 'fried rice,' any local version was usually tasty and filling. What they served here at the embassy was a mild version compared to the local stuff. The Thai's like everything spiced so hot it would, as Stony once observed, "Set a Mexican bandit's mouth on fire." He ordered his accompanied by a couple of "Green Spot" orange drinks.

He ate alone; it was a little early for the lunch crowd. Stony had never felt comfortable at forced conversation and it was the accepted practice that during the lunch hour when seats were scarce, you took any empty chair. Problem was, you were expected to actually talk to the other people. He had developed the habit of trying to eat early or late.

As he re-entered the office he could see JJ was at his desk, visibly fuming as he studied a briefing paper. He glared at Stony, then fired an angry glance towards Allan's office and continued reading. They must have had a good row, Stony figured, and knowing Allan, he probably threw tonight's assignment at JJ like a weapon. Stony and JJ had worked together several times over the years. They knew and trusted each other. JJ was a straight arrow but he did like to drink a little too much and sometimes got real ornery when he did. He lived alone, having sent his family home due to the kids' severe allergies to everything in the tropics. Lately, as Stony's time to leave grew threateningly closer, JJ had been putting a lot of his own time into the investigation, without admitting it, of course. It was part loyalty and part just being a street agent. Espionage was funny that way, so many things interrelated. Stony and JJ knew their element and liked it. Assignments cam down from above of course, but street agents had a certain feel for the medium. It's what made it all work.

Promptly at 1900 hours, Stony and JJ boarded the helicopter atop the embassy. It was a UH-1D "Huey," the workhorse of the Vietnam era. As they strapped in, JJ leaned over to Stony, "This chopper jockey looks like a teenager."

With a sudden movement the chopper lifted off the helipad, banking so sharply that they were staring straight at the ground.

"Flies like one too!"

CHAPTER 3

The chopper climbed into the evening sky and the embassy compound withdrew rapidly. The sprawling city was already well lit, especially the multi-colored business signs of the entertainment districts. The main streets were rivers of headlights. He tried to find his house but couldn't and soon the bright city lights disappeared behind them.

The flight was short, just under an hour, and the chopper didn't fly very high. As a kid back in Colorado, Stony wished he could view the country through the eyes of one of the Red-tailed hawks as they soared lazily through the high plains summer sky. So in spite of the limited light, he was enjoying the flight. The land below them was flat and they could see far to the east and west until the jungle disappeared into the humidity. Below them he could still make out small farm clearings, several villages and lots of waterways. He could barely see farmers coming in from their rice paddies, kids bringing in groups of water buffalo and watercraft gliding along the canals. Then the light faded rapidly as it does in the tropics. They flew along the highway south out of Bangkok and were soon over the Gulf of Thailand. It wasn't long before he could see, off to the left, the lights of the beach resort town of Pattaya, which brought back family memories of weekend getaways. Then they dropped to the designated helipad at Sattihip, the large Thai-American airbase which is on a corner of the bay as the land takes a sharp left turn towards Cambodia.

The jet was ready, according to plan. It wasn't a large craft, just a VIP transport, capable of holding about a dozen individuals and comfortably outfitted, as you would expect. After the DC-3's and C130's he had flown on recently, this one seemed liked a sports car and flew like one too. In no time they were high in the sky, zipping along. The flight into South Vietnam was short, about 45 minutes through the night sky. They flew high and fast as was the custom over South Vietnam, to avoid anti-aircraft fire, and then nose-dived onto the runway, leveling off just prior to touchdown for the same reason.

"Who-eee! That's better than a country fair roller-coaster!" whistled Stony as they taxi'd to a stop.

"Cheap thrills courtesy of your friendly air Force," countered JJ.

They were met by a squad of soldiers. A tall, lean Sergeant with a combat hardened face handed them flak jackets and jungle fatigues.

"Chopper's over here sirs, ready to go. I'm Sergeant McDaniels and I'll brief you during the flight."

Stony and JJ donned the flak jackets over their already dark clothes; it was too hot to add the fatigues. Stony adjusted his Smith and Wesson 38 for easy access. Once strapped into the Huey with headsets on, they were briefed by Sergeant McDaniels in his deep southern accent.

"Your target is approximately nine minutes north, northwest. We'll come in low and set down in a clearing about half a mile to the southeast of the village. The jungle should muffle our arrival. Sergeant Matthews, our radioman, says your man is on the air right now, so you might catch him in the act. We'll escort you to the hut we have previously indentified, wait nearby out of sight and escort you back again. If you don't see us, just proceed southeast, we'll be there."

At the site the chopper hovered just above the ground. The group dropped out quickly and silently and headed for the bush. The chopper disappeared into the night sky. They trekked noiselessly along a narrow jungle path for awhile and once in the village proceeded quickly but cautiously. It was a small village, deep in the Mekong River valley, very dark and mostly quiet. The night sky offered only slight illumination. Somewhere a dog barked briefly. The ground had been muddied by a recent rain. The pungent odor of supper fires and wet thatch hung in the air. Some of the houses were made of corrugated metal and wood, some had thatch roofs. The target hut was entirely thatch.

After checking it out, Stony and JJ stepped quietly into the dimly lit hut, weapons drawn. JJ spotted and quickly lifted a trap door. In a pit, not three feet across, using a hand generated transmitter and radio, illuminated by a small red light, sat the VC operator. He looked up in stark terror and grabbed madly for his pistol. Stony fired twice, the blasts shattering the silence, both rounds into the VC's forehead, even though the VC's head had jerked back violently with the first shot. He slumped straight down; there was nowhere else for his body to go in the narrow hole, blood dripping off his head. JJ reached in, pulled the equipment more or less into a pile and ignited the grenade. He lowered the trap door and they hastily departed. The war-wearied villagers offered no reaction, although they would soon have a fire to fight. As they slipped out of the village JJ whispered, "They cremate over here anyway, don't they? By the way, lucky second shot."

As Stony looked back, he could see the growing fire from the hut. He hoped the recent rain would keep it from spreading and give the villagers a break.

They quietly backtracked and met up with the squad just outside the village. Link up and lift off went smoothly, but not for long. The Huey lurched. Sergeant McDaniels drawled into the headphones, "Pilot says we've been hit by ground fire. There's a Fire Support Base about six clicks south, we're gonna make for it. Hang On!"

The chopper's motor began to sound pretty rough and even in the barely lit night sky; Stony could see and smell the black, oily plume they were emitting.

As they approached the FSB, Sergeant McDaniels came over the headset again. "It's being shelled but we're going in anyway. Better to go down inside there than anywhere around it. When we hit the ground, bale out on the run and head down the ramp for cover."

Stony could see the Fire Support Base from his perch behind the door gunner. It was larger than he had imagined and was being shelled pretty hard. Dust and smoke filled the air, illuminated by numerous flares. The helipad was just visible off toward the center of the compound. To the west appeared to be a runway, although it was hard to be sure through all the smoke. He could barely make out a couple of fighter-bombers doing a job on the VC.

The chopper shuddered in at treetop level, made it to the helipad with difficulty, and pancaked hard to the ground. Everybody split downhill and dove into bunkers. It sounded like all hell was breaking loose. The pilot was last out and was hit by ground fire. Two soldiers ran back, grabbed him and dragged him downhill on the run. Medics said it wasn't too bad, they would handle it. One of the Special Forces sergeants informed a nearby captain that Stony and JJ were civilians and the captain led them into a deeper bunker and sat down for a moment on a stack of ammo boxes. He took off his helmet, sat it on the ground and wiped his sweating forehead with a dirty tan handkerchief. He was younger than Stony and JJ, maybe late twenties, thinning hair above a tanned and tired but earnest face.

"Been shelling us since just after dark. We're pretty well dug in here, don't expect much damage. Fun starts when they quit. Then they hit us. They'll use the shelling to get in position. Hopefully our air-strikes will hurt 'em some." He turned to depart when JJ grabbed his arm.

"Mister, er, Captain, Stony and I may not be soldiers but we're both pretty good shots. And besides, should you lose, I don't intend to be gunned down in some hole like a rat."

Stony added, "If you could spare a couple of M16's and helmets, we'd just as soon be on the line. We've both been in the Army when we were younger. I believe we could be of some use up there."

"Sir, you're civilians, if the press ever got hold of this my career would go straight down the tube," answered the Captain.

JJ grabbed the Captain's arm, "We're Americans first, Captain. Besides, we're both intelligence agents and we trade shots with Commie's every day. Just give us a couple M16's and if you see any reporters out there, I'll shoot the son of a bitch myself."

The Captain grimaced and looked about to turn them down, then he grinned, "What the hell, why not."

As he was leaving, JJ shouted, "Remember the Alamo!"

"What the hell was that for?" laughed Stony. JJ just shrugged.

Sometime around 0300 the shelling stopped. Stony and JJ took up perimeter positions as instructed. Suddenly the sky was alive with flares in a rough circle around the firebase. Stony glanced around to orient himself. The FSB seemed to cover the top of a relatively flat hill. Probably bulldozed flat by military engineers. They were on the southern end of the base. Sandbagged Conex's and bunkers all over the place. Over to his right he could see the end of a landing strip. The area in front of him had been cleared of vegetation for a few hundred yards or so down to the brush, although there were a couple of gullies within his field of fire. He hoped they had been mined. The air was thick with dust and the smell of explosives. Brief firefights broke out first in one area and then another. Evidently the VC unit wasn't large enough to risk a frontal assault and was content to launch probes, searching for a vulnerable area to breach. Several times the fighting became intense and more air-strikes were called in. Stony and JJ kept their eyes roving, knowing that if you stare at something long enough in limited light, it will not only seem to move but might even dance for you. The adrenaline was high this night, the shelling and small arms fire almost constant, often drowning out the roar of the jets on their strikes.

Shots tore into the sandbags just below Stony's face. He fired several rounds at the muzzle flares, none returned.

"Something's going on out there, Stony," it was JJ, "I think we're about to get it."

Suddenly machine-gun fire raked their position. Everybody ducked. A mortar round exploded behind them, then another. Then one out in front. Small arms fire erupted all around. Everybody firing! The VC was hard to see in those black pajamas. Must be hundreds of them! More flares, explosions, yelling, screaming, rifle fire, more noise than he thought his ears could stand. Something hit his helmet so hard it snapped his head back, vision blurred, "shake it off, keep firing, quit and you die, reload, keep firing, keep firing, they're falling back, don't let up, that one's alive – shoot him again, keep firing."

And then it was over.

They were gone, melted away into the brush. Black clad bodies littered the field to their front. He watched for movement. They hadn't gotten closer than about 30 yards. That was close enough! He turned and slumped to the ground.

"JJ! You ok?"

"Right here. Jeez, Stony, looks like you took one to the head. You alright?"

"Vision was a little blurred for awhile. I'm alright now."

Stony glanced to his left, "Looks like everybody wasn't so lucky. The lieutenant here's got a bad one. MEDIC! OVER HERE!"

The medic slid down beside the lieutenant, "We've got this one, how about that one over there?"

JJ crawled over to the soldier laying face down. He felt for a pulse, and then rolled him over. Stony heard JJ mutter something, and then he heard him getting sick. He waived the medic off and crawled back.

"Sorry, I wasn't ready for that. Half his face is gone. I closed his other eye and then I lost it. Sorry."

They each stared for a long moment at the ground, then returned to their posts behind the sandbagged wall. At the first hint of daylight the firing stopped. An eerie quiet descended over the hilltop.

A soldier yelled, "Sergeant! Over here!"

"Oh great!" was the reply.

Barely visible in the limited light was a dark figure on a bicycle, slowly pedaling up towards them on a narrow path. She was wearing a loose fitting dark blouse and pants, with a conical flat-brimmed straw hat on her head. It was the normal clothing of a Vietnamese villager. She seemed to be approaching at a measured pace, at least that was Stony's impression.

"It's a woman," someone yelled.

"What's the problem?" asked JJ.

"My guess is it's a bike bomb. I can't believe they're trying this." answered the Sergeant. "They're gambling we won't shoot her. You shoot a civilian anymore and your ass is grass."

The girl was about a hundred yards out now, still coming. The sun wasn't up yet; the dim light was filled with smoke and haze which wafted over her occasionally giving her a ghostly countenance. Tension mounted. The girl peddled slowly closer, occasionally steering around a corpse. Stony looked at the soldiers around him. He suspected they were weighing court-martial against survival, the higher the rank, the more the risk.

He began sighting her with his M16. "I believe in doing dangerous things carefully. If she is a bike bomb, we're all dead." They couldn't evacuate, they had to defend their position. Several soldiers began to yell at her, some in Vietnamese.

She wasn't fifty yards away. He sighted her carefully. Despite the drifting smoke, he could see her features clearly now in the early morning light. She was sort of attractive. He felt terrible. He knew she didn't want to be here anymore than he did. He knew he would never forget her face. She seemed to be looking right into his eyes. He aimed just between hers and slowly pulled the trigger. The rifle kicked, a small red splotch appeared just above the bridge of her nose. Time froze. She didn't move, just sat there on her bike, looking straight at him, and then she slowly began to fall to her left side. She fell to the ground and just laid there. Just laid there. He felt confused, maybe even guilty, maybe she really was innocent.

JJ body-blocked him to the ground just as an ear-penetrating explosion ripped the air.

"Sirs", it was Sergeant McDaniels, "they're bringing in more troops; we can hitch a ride out on one of the return choppers."

The Sergeant began rounding up his squad and they proceeded through the carnage down to the landing strip. Several choppers were off loading troops and taking on wounded.

Stony turned to JJ, "Sure, we get to go home. These guys gotta do this all over again tonight."

They both took a long, slow look around at the tired, the dead, and the wounded, the dust and the smoke, and handed their weapons to a nearby sergeant. Stony felt a little guilty about leaving.

Once on the jet back to Thailand, the adrenaline began to wane and fatigue set in. The seats were comfortable but the ride was choppy. They fought sleep and their silences weren't helping.

"So much for the Colonel's scheduling," quipped Stony.

"Bet you feel like you've been rode hard and put away wet, eh cowboy?"

"That's an old, worn-out cliché, JJ."

"Well, things get to be clichés because they ring true, Stony."

"You got a point, ol' buddy. But what I'm thinking right now is that I'd give 50 bucks for a big plate of huevos."

"A big plate of what?"

"Huevos Rancheros. Mexican ranch eggs." Stony smiled. JJ knew he liked his Mexican food. Nodding his head, Stony stared upwards at nothing in particular.

"Best I ever had was in a little place in Pagosa Springs, Colorado. Came down Wolf Creek Pass pulling two horses in a stock trailer, clutch gave out and my brakes overheated. What a ride! First open garage was in Pagosa Springs. I guess anything would have tasted good that morning – I thought for sure I was going to be eating asphalt and pine trees."

"So what are they like?" JJ shifted his position, leaning out into the isle.

"Once in a while I'll make them for Sunday brunch at the ranch. I pile taco-flavored ground beef on a big flour tortilla, layer on a three egg omelet, and top it with lettuce, chopped onion, cheddar cheese, and a liberal dose of picante sauce."

JJ snapped back into his seat, throwing his hands upwards, "Damn it Stony, knock it off. I'm already starvin' and now you've got my mouth waterin' and my stomach growlin'."

"You asked."

"You gotta think about your ranch, think of some of the crap jobs, like branding or something."

"Branding a crap job? I can tell you've never been to a branding, JJ. Let me tell you how it goes at our place. We usually only tell a few neighbors, who come over and help, and then we return the favor to them. If we let the word get out, we'd have every nightclub cowboy in the country out there, getting in the way and getting hurt. It sure ain't no crap job, JJ. For some of us it's the highlight of late spring."

"Hell, Stony, I don't know anything about cows. When I've seen it in the movies, it seems just a way to get beat up and dirty. How come you think it's so great?" He was leaning towards Stony again.

"Well, probably because it's like an athletic event and a festival all in one. At least it is the way we do it. We usually round up the cattle the afternoon before and leave 'em in the corral overnight. At dawn the mother cows are more than willing to get back to grass so it's easier to separate the calves off. We do it slow and easy, no rodeo-ing, we want to keep the dust down and the calves as calm as possible. That way we don't hurt animals or people."

"Next, we need a real good crew, because if you've got one, you can average a calf a minute. We run about two hundred head and we're usually done in less than four hours. A healer ropes their hind legs and pulls them over to the branding crew. One guy flanks them, and then holds the head down and grabs the front legs. We brand, inoculate against a number of diseases, and castrate the steers, all in about a minute or so. We do it so fast the calf hardly knows what's happening before it's turned loose again. We don't hurry the job; it's just that practiced hands make short work of it. We've usually got it all done and the calves mothered up by lunch. Then we break out the beer. Meanwhile, my wife and the other ladies bring out the bar-b-que beef, buckets of pinto beans and baked potatoes, and if anybody has room, there's usually several home-baked pies and coffee. I usually don't get to the pies 'til much later. My wife's bar-b-que sauce was so good; some people would just eat it with a spoon, and I was one of them. We've got several Mexican-American neighbors and like as not they'd bring their guitars. It always turned out to be a big fiesta."

"There you go again – talking about food."

"You asked, again."

"I got to admit, the way you describe it, it does sound like a good time. Damn, I'm hungry."

To change the subject, they planned their moves for the delivery of the small fortune to the Chinats the following night. Their return connections went smoothly and they arrived back at the embassy at 8:15 am, descended the helipad to the third floor and stopped by the office. The cover music that was played in the entrance booth to deter eavesdropping had changed from easy listening to rock and roll.

"Guess who's back?" said JJ.

Pete Finch and John Elmsly were the other team in the office. A good five years younger than Stony and JJ, they were faster paced, almost hyper. They were a real Mutt and Jeff team, Pete was just over six feet, with a full head of blonde hair and slender. John was much shorter, with dark brown receding hair, a full mustache, a small paunch and a decidedly jovial demeanor. They all got along great; it was just that their approach to things was different. Such as to the boss. Stony and JJ tried to maintain a cordial distance, difficult as that could be at times. Pete and John, on the other hand, pretended a certain camaraderie while playing horrendous practical jokes on him. Allan accepted this toying because he seemed convinced, in his own pompous way that it made him 'one of the boys.'

Pete and John had just returned from a little trip into Vientiane, Laos.

"Bon jour, mon ami." quipped JJ in his best French accent.

"Please cut the French crap. We're all Frenched out," shot back John.

"Those Frenchies sure left their mark on Vientiane." answered Pete, who was typing up his report in his rapid two-finger style.

"Everyplace had only French food or something unrecognizable. I'd even have welcomed some Thai fried rice."

"Yea, some good ol' kow pot." chimed John as he refilled his coffee cup.

"But did you get the job done?" asked Stony in a mocking reproach.

"Hey! You're talking to the masters," answered Pete.

"Say, you guys joining the rest of us Saturday night? It's time for a boys' night out. We need a ripsnorter," yelled John.

"Everybody?" sneered JJ, glancing towards Allan's smoke filled office.

"Every swinging mother's son," answered John.

"We understand you boys are busy Friday night and we've got to service those horny spouses tonight," said Pete, making an obscene gesture.

"Pete, you're crude as hell. Your wife ever heard you talk like that, she'd cut you off forever," said JJ. "You're the horny one because those cute little sarongs up there turned you on."

Pete stood up and headed towards the coffee pot, "You know, whoever invented those sarongs was a pure genius. They cover a girl from waist to ankle and still don't hide a damn thing, and they don't wear nothin' under 'em at all, you know."

"Hoowee!" cut in John, shoving his chair back against the wall, "Did I ever tell you guys about my first assignment with Pete a few years ago? Talk about crude and horny! We left this bar in a downtown Saigon pretty swacked and were heading for our hotel when Pete spies these two garbage picker girls down an alley." Over the shouted objections of Pete, John continues, "These two broads were bent double, half in and half out of these barrels. "Ol' Pete here, eases up to one of them, slips some money down into the barrel, pulls her sarong up and bangs away. Right there in the alley. Hell, even drunk, I couldn't believe what I was seeing. And, when he finishes, he just pulls the sarong back down, pats her on the butt and strolls off grinning."

"Aw, you're just sore 'cause you were too drunk to approach the other young lady," Pete answered in mock indignation. "Besides, you ain't no saint either. Boys, it wasn't two nights later, I come into my room to find the ugliest whore I ever saw laying in my bed. She says my friend John just left."

John is staggering with laughter, "Hell, she was so ugly, I sure didn't want to screw her in my own bed."

These guys never quit, thought Stony, but they sure do liven up the place.

"Didn't expect you fellows in this morning," said Allan as he refilled his coffee cup and lit another cigarette.

"Just got back. Ran into a little trouble. We're heading home for a little sack time," answered Stony as he and JJ left.

It may have been rude, but he was tired and didn't care to field any questions from the bureaucrat. On the way, he stopped at the Imperial for a cheeseburger to go and ate it as he crawled through the sweltering traffic towards home. He wished he had air-conditioning in this old car.

Only two blocks up Sukhumvit Road, he ran into one of the frustrating phenomena of Bangkok. At the train crossing a freight train was slowly rumbling by. An impatient driver wheeled out and increased the three lanes of traffic to four. He was followed by another. Then a sixth lane formed and a seventh. Stony was well aware that the same thing was happening on the other side of the crossing. He mentally resigned himself to the imminent rodeo.

Eventually the train passed and the traffic arms lifted to find the entire street filled with cars facing each other. Since Thais seem to believe that cars don't run well unless the horn is blowing, the stifling heat erupted with a blaring cacophony. In America fights would have broken out everywhere, but these easy going people probably enjoyed all this as just a break in an otherwise uneventful day.

Stony lived on a short, private street. Three modern, verandah'd houses on each side, built for, and rented to foreigners. There was a small guardhouse at the entrance to the street, but usually no guard was present. It was a common set-up in Bangkok. Most foreigners either lived like this or in apartment compounds. Each house was surrounded by an eight-foot chain-link fence, including a driveway gate, to discourage thieves. Jack Leeds, a Britisher, supposedly in the Import/Export business lived across the narrow street; an Air-America pilot lived next door, an

Australian business man across the street and the other two were French or Belgians or something, he never saw them.

As he eased the bulky '59 Dodge, a replacement car, around the narrow corner, the maid ran out to open the driveway gate. He wasn't comfortable about that, but it was one of the few jobs she had to do anymore. He had kept her on so someone could watch the place and because she had been a good maid when the family had been there. The kids still sent her an occasional photograph. He trusted her. Even hired her husband as the gardener, although the yard was tiny, so they could stay together as a family. They lived in the back, in decent quarters, and Stony found occasional reasons for bonuses. He kept a wary eye on the husband though. He had a bad temper and occasionally got to be too much for the wife. Stony remembered the time last year when the little guy got so mad at his wife he chased her into the house with a machete. She ran upstairs where Stony's wife and children happened to be. The maid charged into the bathroom and locked the door. Stony's wife put the children behind her and met the gardener at the top of the stairs. He had hesitated momentarily and she demanded he hand over the knife. He was so taken aback, that he did. She told Stony later it must have been the children in danger that motivated her, because when the gardener left the house, her knees were so weak, she had to sit down on the floor. Stony's eyes watered at the memory.

From the carport, Stony entered through the kitchen, which was just an alcove off the large main room of the first floor. When he had sent the kids home, he had also sent almost all the furniture and personal belongings. Now the living-dining area held just a couple rattan and pillow easy chairs next to a matching coffee table. Over near one wall was the bar, with its three bar stools. He really didn't have much use for it, but couldn't see any reason for sending it back to Colorado. He headed upstairs, where the three bedrooms and a sitting room were, which except for the main bedroom were also empty. He lived like a monk, having little interest in the house anymore.

This bedroom held only a double bed, a small bureau, some exercise equipment and the window air-conditioner. The bath was off this room.

He showered and stepped into the only air-conditioned room in the house, the bedroom. It actually felt chilly to his wet skin. There was a note to call Jack Leeds, his British neighbor, at the office. He did. Leeds insisted he meet him at the Fasching party, sort of a German Mardi Gras, being held at the Derby Club, this evening. Stony reluctantly agreed, reading something in Leeds manner. Then into welcome slumber.

Unfortunately, although he was exhausted, Stony's biological clock wasn't willing to surrender to a great deal of daytime sleep, so after a few fitful hours he sat up and read a western novel for awhile. He drifted off now and then, and finally, after a brief dream about his wife, he sat on the edge of the bed and tried to sort things out. He was well aware of a creeping despondency beginning to get the upper hand because of his failure to find her killers. He felt he was failing her, the kids, and himself.

He had only taken this job because cattle prices had dipped dangerously low and a local two-year drought had brought him close to losing the ranch. His agency monitor, Richard, had offered a two-year stint in Bangkok. The family thought it would be a great adventure, and if they spent carefully they could come back in good financial shape. They leased the ranchland to his brother, who also agreed to look after the house, and moved to Thailand. Six months into the assignment his wife had been killed by a car bomb meant for him. He had sent the kids, Clancy and Rose Ann, home to his brother for safekeeping. With the help of Richard, his Agency monitor, and over the stringent objections of the Chief of Station, Allan Huehner, he had managed to stay on, vowing to find his wife's killers. It had been a year now, and he was still chasing dead ends. Despite his best efforts, and those of a few friends, he was no closer than ever to finding the killers. He had probed in every conceivable direction. He had done a job on the Burmese early on, but then it might be those who were aware of the Chinat efforts, or the Viets or the Chicoms, or even someone from the past. He had done several jobs for the agency over the years. It was so frustrating. Even Allan was a problem. Initially he had tried to convince Stony to leave by drowning him with assignments. He had Stony's and the kids' best interest at heart, Stony felt, but his interference was tough to take. Before his wife's death, they had been pretty fair friends. Not particularly close, but Allan was a lonely guy and Stony figured he liked visiting with his wife, one of the few American women he could talk to, since he had irritated the rest by hitting on them. He would often come home to find Allan wanting to go out for a drink or whatever.

Afterwards, Allan's attitude changed. He was sure Stony's effectiveness would be severely hindered, that he would get himself killed, that a murder investigation should be left to the authorities, and he has done whatever he could to compel Stony to go home. Also, being a card-carrying CYA bureaucrat, he was probably worried Stony would do something that would endanger his job.

"I've spent a year chasing dead ends, something's got to break, and soon. What the hell am I going to do? I've just got six months left over here and that ain't much time, since I've blown a year already." He realized he was talking out loud to himself.

CHAPTER 4

Stony decided on a little workout to ease the stress. He hooked his feet under the bed and did some sit-ups. His life had been one of physical activity; haying, building fence, feeding cattle, riding, etc. This job didn't provide much exercise so he had purchased a small hundred pound weight set and a bench. They were setup in his bedroom and with the air-conditioning he could get in a pretty decent workout. He had an athlete's build with strong working man hands. Usually easy going, he did have a temper when riled, and he had that typical western 'can do' attitude. After an hour of all this, he felt much better, took a shower and left. It was just before six o'clock in the evening.

As he slowly drove down the crowded boulevard of Sukhumvit Road he thought to himself how this tropical heat and humidity sure was a long way from the cool, dry plains of eastern Colorado.

There were many good restaurants in Bangkok, but tonight he drove straight to the Siam Intercontinental Hotel. One of the most beautiful settings in the city, especially in this twilight. The Intercon, as everyone called it, sat well back from Rama 1 Road in a lavishly landscaped garden. Although the rooms were in a typical boxlike building, the rest of the facilities were centered in and around a magnificent pagoda-like structure which exuded tropical luxury. His family had stayed here when they arrived in Bangkok and between the pool and the small zoo located in the park-like garden out back; it wasn't easy getting the kids to leave when they found a house. Ah, the pool. The PANAM stewardesses stayed at the Intercon between flights in the area, and coupled with their beauty was their fad, at the time, of wearing little handmade crocheted bikinis. And from the looks of the swimsuits, some of those girls quit crocheting just as soon as they could. He remembered tipping the pool waiter five dollars for permanent access to a poolside recliner. Come to think of it, he hadn't wanted to move to the house either.

He parked the car and strolled placidly towards the restaurant via the covered walkway. Off to his left, he could see several people standing around the pool in tropical whites, sipping drinks. The underwater lights were on, illuminating several swimmers whose drinks were parked poolside.

The restaurant was spacious but privacy was assured by the many decorative tropical plants. As the Maître d' led him to a table, he spoke to several acquaintances, but he preferred to dine alone.

In the restaurant Stony declined the appetizer and ordered the specialty of the house, prime rib. He chose a half-bottle of Bordeaux to accompany it. A couple of jobs in Europe had introduced him to wine with dinner and it had become sort of a routine. He had formed the habit of eating his meat well done back in Colorado, "just to make sure everything in it is dead." The wine was cooled just right. He never did understand why people thought red wine should be at room temperature. It tasted a good deal better slightly cooled. Someone once told him that serving at room temperature was a European custom, and if it was, they should have pointed out that European rooms were usually cool, at least those where the wine was stored. He wasn't a connoisseur, but he hated seeing those trendy wine-racks sitting in hot American kitchens.

After a leisurely dinner, which he felt he deserved, he arrived at the Derby Club just after 8 pm. The Derby was a membership club. Not exclusive, just nominally private to give its patrons a refuge from the raucous R&R crowd. The clientele was mostly foreigners on long term duty in Bangkok, and their guests. It was a popular nightspot with a very talented three piece band and a pretty British singer. This week, for added draw the club had been turned into a German beer hall for the annual Fasching festival, with colorful banners, streamers and balloons, and a heavy emphasis on polka music. The normal tables and chairs had been replaced with sturdy picnic type tables with their attached benches. They had to be sturdy because several times a night, the whole crowd snake-danced around and over them.

Stony joined his neighbor Jack at the slightly elevated bar, the better to watch the controlled pandemonium as the band played and the crowd snake-danced. As he mounted a barstool the bartender slid an Amarit beer into his hand.

"Jolly good, Stony. We're in luck. A chap I wanted you to see is here tonight." Leeds leaned in close as he spoke. "Burmese fellow, rather large, ostensibly in the Import/Export business. Nice cover." Leeds was a typical dapper Englishman, neat to a fault, cultured and proper, except sometimes with friends. He spoke with a clipped

British accent that Stony liked to listen to. Stony casually scanned the gyrating crowd.

"He and a woman were sitting just off to the right earlier. I'll point him out when the dance is over. The thing is, he just returned to Bangkok after disappearing about a year ago. Understand?"

Stony understood. After an extended time, the band ended the dance and took a break. Everyone found their previous locations.

"So what do you hear from the little ones, Stony?" Leeds asked as he cued Stony with his gaze.

Stony followed the look and located the Burmese guy sitting with a stunningly beautiful woman wearing what seemed to be a well-fitting, low-cut bodysuit or dress. She also looked to be Burmese.

"Got a letter two days ago. Been snowing back there. I think they are wearing out my brother's snowmobiles. Both doing well in school. Get a letter every week. Really miss them." He took a long drink from his mug.

"I imagine so. Must be difficult."

There was a commotion near the bandstand as a group of visiting Germans hustled a table up front and prevailed upon the bandleader, an Austrian, who was also part owner, to hold a beer drinking contest. He issued the challenge and three heavy, beaming Germans bounded to the front. They, and incidentally, the whole four-piece band, were each wearing colorful German shirts and lederhosen, those knee-length leather shorts so common in Germany. They seemed in great spirits.

The Burmese guy, a big stout fellow himself, got up and joined them. There was some hearty handshaking all around and a waiter brought each of then a quart sized mug of beer.

The bandleader signaled go, the drummer played a flourish, and the guzzling commenced. The Burmese guy downed his first, hardly spilling a drop, and slammed his mug down hard on the table, just ahead of one of the Germans, who in a rush had spilled some beer down his shirt. The other two were a sloppy third and fourth. The bandleader held up the Burmese's hand, declaring him the winner. Having an oriental outdo Germans in a beer drinking contest didn't sit well with the crowd. They were on their feet protesting loudly while the three on the floor were threatening violence. Finally, the bandleader worked out a compromise. The fastest German and the Burmese would engage in an immediate rematch. Two more quart mugs of beer were brought forward. The two losers loudly cheered their man on, the signal was given, the drummer played another flourish, and once again, hardly spilling a drop, the Burmese guzzled his beer and slammed the empty mug down on the table first. The German was wearing much of his beer as he tried to hurriedly pour too much into his mouth and slammed his mug down, still a quarter full. Looking about to burst, he sped toward the men's room. His crowd was on its feet again, shouting and throwing a few coasters, they started forward.

Stony strode quickly forward and stood with the Burmese man. Another man did the same. Several in the crowd stood up. The Germans got the message. They began to quiet down; the bandleader said something to them in German, they appeared chastened. He turned and congratulated the Burmese, presenting him with a Thai hundred baht note as his prize.

Stony returned to his barstool. The band played the first of three temperament calming slow dances.

"Riding to the rescue, cowboy?" joked Leeds.

Stony grinned, "They were clearly wrong. Probably good guys, just too much beer and wounded pride. Besides, if the Burmese fellow is our man, I could be playing mind-games with him."

"Well, old boy, you are about to get another chance."

Stony turned as the Burmese gentleman and his lady approached. He was a big barrel-chested, dark-skinned man, with a heavy mass of oiled, coal black hair, slightly taller and a great deal larger than Stony. She was an absolute beauty, lighter skinned, deep, dark eyes, long raven hair, wearing a skintight sky-blue low-cut, body hugging mini-dress that left absolutely nothing to the imagination.

"I want to thank you for standing up for me. I am Ba Maung and this is my wife, Mai. I am in the Import/Export business, my card." They all shook hands. Maung spoke with a definite British accent, probably schooled in England.

"Stony McGraw, American Embassy, no card. And it was no problem, they were wrong, you were right."

"We would like to invite you to dinner. We are on our way now."

"Thank you all the same, Mr. Maung, but I just came from dinner."

"Another time then. Perhaps we could have lunch sometime?"

Stony's gut tightened. Something told him not to lose this guy.

"Alright. How about tomorrow, the Intercon at noon. Great cheeseburgers," answered Stony.

"Tomorrow then. Now if you will excuse me," he grinned, "I must visit the water closet immediately." He turned and walked quickly away. Stony lightly touched the lady's arm, "Madame Maung, would you care to dance while we wait?"

The band had started the second slow dance. She danced close to him, very close. With her arm around his waist, she pulled herself tight, sensually tight. "Damn," he mused, "she's riding my leg!" Her every movement was subtly erotic. Not a word was spoken between them. When the music stopped, she looked into his eyes and took her time letting go. Afterward he returned her to the waiting husband. He thanked her and they left for their dinner.

"Whoa! That is one fine body. And the way she dances. She must be the reason they call slow dances 'the rubs.' said Stony as he reached for his beer.

"She was certainly painted into that mini-dress. Now what you need is a cold shower," Leeds said as he laughed and slid off his barstool, "Well, my work here is done. Good night, Stony."

Stony remained on his barstool. The earlier wine, delicious dinner, the beer and the tiger lady, sort of combined themselves and he decided to just sit in the glow awhile. And what about this Burmese guy. He could be the reason every other lead had led nowhere. He left about a year ago. Maybe he was back because he figured Stony would no longer be in Bangkok. Then again, maybe he's back to finish the job. This could be it. Finally he could settle the score. He sipped his beer, cautiously elated.

An unordered beer was set in front of him. He glanced at the bartender questionably; who nodded towards Stony's left. He turned searchingly and his eyes met those of a beautiful Amer-Asian lady, probably in her twenties, seated at a table in the back, alone. She smiled. He motioned a thank you. Just then three young American men descended on her table, probably someone's guests, obviously in a party mood. The lady wasn't smiling. Plaintively, she looked again at Stony.

Stony put down his beer, walked over to her table, leaned down and asked her to dance. Wordlessly she rose.

"Sorry boys," he said to the disappointed trio as he led her to the dance floor.

"That is the second time tonight you have come to someone's rescue," she whispered as they danced. Stony was mentally thankful for the band's timing, they had just begun another slow dance.

"No big deal. Besides I was considering asking you to dance, it's just, well; I haven't asked a strange lady to dance in a lot of years."

"And you did that for a second time tonight also."

"You don't miss much do you?"

She was a smooth, practiced dancer. He inhaled her exotic perfume as he held her tender little hand in his. They danced close, but nothing like the tiger lady. He had noticed her at the club before, on several occasions, usually alone, well dressed, striking figure, long dark hair, and great legs, - Stony was a leg man. In keeping with the current fashion, she was wearing a tight fitting, light rose, Thai-silk mini-dress with matching high heels, no nylons. Her beautifully shaped, light tan legs didn't need them. After the dance, he returned her to her table, and thanked her for the beer and the dance.

"Would you like to sit down," she asked, "we could talk?"

A waiter brought over his beer, he ordered another Mai Tai for her. Maybe she wanted him to run interference in case the party boys returned. It didn't really matter, he liked her company.

"They call me Stony."

"I am Som-Marie."

"That's a real pretty name. Kinda unusual, isn't it?"

"Thai and American. My father was with the American Consulate; my mother taught at the university." She was very intelligent with a great command of English.

"I was very impressed with your bravery tonight. You could've been hurt."

"It was no big deal. I just didn't like the odds. Those were probably just good ol' boys with too much to drink." He changed the subject. "Say, I'm not much of a dancer but I can handle this one. Would you care to try it again?" She did. Thankfully the band was playing a couple of slow dances between polkas, probably to give the customers and them a chance to rest, and of course, to order more drinks.

Just before midnight she asked if he would like to go somewhere for coffee. He did. She knew just the place and for him to follow her. She pulled out from the parking lot behind the building in a white American convertible, top down, her long ebony hair flowing in the breeze. He followed. They drove up Sukhumvit, past his own street, past the tall, almost finished Chokechai building, past the pocket markets, and into a narrow, dimly lit lane. She slowed and turned towards an iron-gated residence compound. A sleeping Indian guard slowly aroused himself and opened the gate. Stony smiled as he thought about this ridiculous setup. The guard was supposed to be the security for the compound, so he would string a hammock across the entrance gate and sleep in it. Anyone entering had to wake him to get through the gate. This way, he perfunctorily performed his duty. It was a common setup in Bangkok. The problem was the burglars or "stealy boys" never strolled through the gate. Naturally, they just climbed the walls.

Stony followed Som-Marie through the gate and into the park-like walled compound. Inside was a typical living area for better-off Thais, several houses set in garden like surroundings; sort of a manicured estate shared by the owners. They pulled up to the door of a small villa. He followed her inside. It was cool and comfortable. He wished he could say the same about himself. He didn't quite know why, but he was just a little nervous. He pulled off his boots, since it was the local custom, and he wanted to be polite, and he also slipped the left boot's holster down out of site. She motioned him to the couch.

"Please sit down, I will be right back."

Stony figured she was changing into 'something more comfortable,' or maybe she was making coffee. That was why they left the club, wasn't it? The room was sparsely decorated, in the Thai custom. Terrazzo floors, the walls a soft, very light blue with three large Thai temple rubbings adorning them. The temple rubbings were a local art form of their own, made by rubbing the intricate frescoes of the local temples onto thin rice paper with a piece of art charcoal. Inexpensive here, he understood they were worth a great deal back in the states.

"Here you are fresh orange and pineapple juice, with two kinds of rum. Just like at the derby." She handed him a Mai Tai, sipping one of her own. "Sorry, but I don't have any beer."

"Thought we were going for coffee," he suggested lightly.

She sat on the couch close to him, not touching, but close. "You are not relaxed, are you? Is it me?"

"No, no it's not you. It's me. I'm just a little uncomfortable. It's been a long time since I've been out with a woman, you see…" She cut him off.

"I know about you. I know about the terrible thing that happened to your wife. I am very, very sorry about that. If you wish to go, it would be alright," she said it slowly, softly.

He looked deeply into her eyes. He saw compassion, understanding. "I'm sorry. I didn't mean to get heavy tonight. Maybe I should…"

"Did you love her?"

"Very much. Why do you ask that?"

"Because it matters. The way you answered tells me something about you. How long has it been, a year?"

"Just a little over a year."

"Then you have completed the period of mourning," she announced.

"I'll probably never really get to that point," he answered.

She stood, put her drink on the table beside the couch, and walked around behind him. She moved with the grace of a dancer. He wondered how someone so intelligent, so beautiful, so, well, sweet, could still be single. At least he hoped she was single. He hadn't noticed any signs of a man living here anyway. She put her soft hands on his shoulders and slowly moved them to his neck.

"You are very tense, Mister Stony McGraw. You need to relax. I am very good at massage." She said it almost in a whisper, as she gently but firmly stroked his neck muscles. He felt the magic of those fingers beginning to do their job.

"This is not the best place. Come with me, I will make you very relaxed." She came around the couch, took his hand and led the way to the bedroom. There it was dark and cool, the only light coming obliquely from the lamp in the living room. She turned and unbuttoned his shirt. He had his hands on her slim waist. She smiled up at him as she slipped his shirt off his shoulders. She did not offer to kiss him but undid his trousers and held them as he stepped out of them. He had earlier slipped his 38 revolver under the front seat of the car. She led him to the bed, and in a cute touch of formality, "Face down please."

As he lay down on the clean, lavender scented bed, she deftly dropped her Thai silk dress to the floor. She was wearing nothing else. She sat on his ankles and began a systematic massage, beginning with his calves, working upward over his back and ending with his neck and shoulders. She did know massage. Her soft hands were strong and gentle. He began to let go, to really relax. He was swooning in this misty pleasure when she gently lifted his right shoulder, indicating that he should turn over. Sitting on his thighs, she gently but thoroughly worked his chest and stomach, his arms. As he watched her through half opened eyes, he could relish her beautiful, nude body. He lazily observed her well-formed breasts, her soft, tan complexion, and her taut belly. She slid down on his ankles, their eyes met, she smiled.

In his trance-like state Stony began to feel the misty pleasure washed away by onrushing passion, then the urging, surging, throbbing explosion of relief.

And it was over. He felt drained. She disappeared for a moment. When she returned, she pulled a sheet over them both and lay there, half on his body, her head on his shoulder. He lay there, thoroughly relaxed.

In a little while, she rose to lean on her elbow, she kissed him gently on the lips, "Gather your strength, Stony McGraw."

Afterward, they lay there awhile, his arm around her, her head on his shoulder. Comfortable. That was the word, comfortable. For the first time in a long while he didn't feel the stifling weight of his problems. In fact, he felt nothing but the fuzzy, warm enveloping sensation of pleasure.

He awoke to the aroma of fresh coffee. Som-Marie was sitting on the edge of the bed. She smiled, leaned over and kissed him on the forehead.

"I have some fresh melon ready, if you would like."

"What time is t?"

"6:30. Do you have to go?"

"Not yet."

The coffee was not as hot when they got around to it.

"I would like very much to see you again. I would like to get to know you," he said. "How about dinner Sunday."

"Are you sure you wish to be seen with me. Some foreigners seem to think I am a prostitute," she said seriously.

He grinned a silly grin, "Are you a prostitute?"

She returned his grin, "Did I charge you?"

He took her left hand in his own, "Som-Marie, you let me worry about that. I would be proud to be seen with you. How about three Sunday afternoon? Maybe we could see some of the local sights and follow it up with dinner?"

"You like Chinese?"

"It's a date." He kissed her and left for the house.

He kept his appointment with the Burmese guy. Not knowing what might happen, he considered calling the office for backup. But if his men were recognized, it could scuttle everything. He was wearing a light tan short sleeved, straight bottomed shirt, outside his full cut trousers – both meant to conceal his inside the belt holster. Maybe, since he was early, he could position himself to his advantage.

No such luck. As he entered the restaurant at the Intercon, he noticed Maung already there, seated with his back to the wall. Great. Then, without acknowledging him, he noticed his British friend Leeds at another table, carefully screened from Maung by some of the large tropical plants. Leeds had been present at the invitation last night and was acting as backup on his own. It was nice to have friends. Stony approached Maung's table, after patting his 38.

"You're early, Mr. Maung, or am I late?" he inquired casually, as he put out his hand. Maung stood politely.

"Please, just call me Ba, and I am early. I thought traffic would be much worse. I just ordered a Mai Tai, would you care for one?" Stony did.

"They put so much fruit in these; they could double for an appetizer." Stony joked.

The waitress returned for their order.

"What was that you mentioned last night? It sounded as if you endorse something from the menu here," said Maung.

"Cheeseburger," replied Stony, "grilled ground beef, cheese, onion, lettuce and tomato. Great sandwich and this is the best in town."

"I shall try one, on your recommendation."

"Two please, with fries," Stony said to the pretty Thai waitress. They made innocuous small talk while they waited for their order. Stony decided to push things a little.

"It seems that I've seen you before, Ba. Weren't you here in Bangkok a year or so ago?"

"Yes, I was," replied Maung, apparently nonplused. "I was here for a month when my father died. I was forced to return home to handle the arrangements and settle the estate. I could have lived on the inheritance but a man must do something productive. I returned to the Ex-Im business. Presently I am engaged in marketing teak lumber to a concern in Sweden for the production of furniture."

"That's interesting. My wife bought a few pieces of teak last year," said Stony, vainly hoping for some reaction. He was forcing himself to be amiable. If this actually was the hit man, he would rather be ripping his throat out.

"Be very careful when you take it home to the U.S. Teak furniture made here in the tropics has a tendency to split apart once it reaches a more arid climate. Tell your wife to be sure to use plenty of linseed oil on it," said Maung. No reaction whatever.

"Is it in the way they cure it?" asked Stony, figuring he could act as casual as this guy.

"Partially. But then teak is cured differently from other woods. Because its market value is greater than any other wood except mahogany, great care is taken to preserve this value. Did you know that a fresh cut teak log will not float? No, it must first be cured. However, if you fell it and let it cure on the ground, it will cure unevenly. We use an old Burmese method by which we first girdle the tree, you know, a wide strip of bark is removed near its base and then the tree dies. We leave it there, sometimes up to three years, depending on its size. This way it cures itself completely and evenly. Only then do we cut it down," instructed Maung.

"Seems I've seen pictures of the next step. You use elephants to move the logs to the nearest river," mentioned Stony.

"Right you are. The trees grow over a hundred feet tall. We cut them into logs which the elephants drag away to be floated downstream to our facilities. The wood I market comes mainly from northern Thailand. We have much more in Burma, but while the Thai government exercised great control in the interest of conservation, in Burma the government owns everything." He grinned and leaned closer to Stony. "The Burmese way to socialism."

"Must keep you pretty busy," said Stony. He was watching a couple stewardesses walk past in extra short miniskirts.

"Oh. Quite right. Why this very afternoon I am flying to Chaing Mai to handle some arrangements."

"Is that a fact?" said Stony, making a mental note as the food arrived. He reached for his Mai Tai for a long, slow drink, stalling to see how Maung would handle his cheeseburger. His wife had always said he had a little ornery streak in him. Without hesitating, Maung picked up his knife and fork and began cutting his burger into pieces, just as Stony suspected he would.

"Before you mangle that thing too bad, this is the way we eat a cheeseburger," said Stony as he picked his up and took a bite. He figured he may have been a little shy on politeness, but pointing out Maung's minor faux pas may provide a little edge down the line. The meal continued smoothly, with Maung eating his French fries with his fork, Stony, with his fingers. Maung graciously picked up the tab and Stony caught Leeds' eye briefly as they departed. He'd let him know later that he appreciated the backup.

It bothered him that he could get no reaction from Maung. He was suddenly the prime suspect, everything fit. Stony had done a real job on the Burmese early on, in support of the Chinats. When his wife had been killed by the car bomb, meant for him, he figured it was their answer. Maung had left the country about then, although he hadn't been aware of it at the time. Was he really that smooth? Stony had carefully observed his every motion, especially his eyes, but there had been no reaction to his prodding whatsoever. This guy was really good. And why did he just happen to mention that he was going to Chaing Mai this very afternoon? Who was playing mind-games with whom?

He decided to call on an old contact he had used often before. Although he was supposed to be at the Embassy to meet JJ, this little detour wouldn't take long and just might turn up some much needed info. He hung a right on Payatai Road and after a couple of turns he pulled up in front of a decrepit office building. Inside, on the second floor to the rear, he found his man. He knocked on the door, tried the handle and stepped in.

"Hey, Wirey, wake up, you've got a customer."

"I not sleeping, I in deep contemplation." Wirey knew a lot of English, but not a lot of grammar. He stood up and smiling broadly, put out his hand. Mr. Wira Pantasuk, Private Detective, was a small man, but his great horned-rimmed glasses, thinning hair and thoughtful observations, gave him the air of a retired college professor. In fact, "the professor" was the name he was referred to back in the office. Stony just called him Wirey. Very discreet, they used his services whenever a foreigner snooping around would blow things.

"What you need, my friend?" Wirey asked.

"Got a guy I want watched for a few days. Burmese fellow, named Ba Maung. He's supposed to go to Chaing Mai this afternoon, probably on a commercial in-country flight. After that I'm not sure. I just want to know what he does for a few days. Can you handle it?"

"Can handle. Ten dollars every day, American money."

"Sounds reasonable. Here's fifty bucks, I'll get back to you in a few days. Okay?" It was the usual fee.

Okay. Three days, he be open book. Khop Khoon Krop," Wirey replied, closing with the Thai thank you.

Stony retraced his route through the teeming, dusty streets, and in front of the Intercon, turned right, down the cluttered streets of a new shopping district, Siam Square. It was a grid of several blocks of two-story, flat-topped, store-fronted, light-gray, monotonous buildings. More orderly than the other shopping districts, with fewer street stands and sidewalk vendors. It had a more subdued bustle to it, as if consciously trying to imitate an American shopping center.

Stony stopped by a luggage shop and picked up two cheap, non-matching suitcases and proceeded to the Embassy.

At the stoplight on the corner of Vittayu/Wireless Road he was irritated by another local traffic custom. As soon as the light changed, the guy behind him honked his horn. This always pissed him off, but he usually tried to ignore it as everyone else did. This time he didn't. He jumped out of his car, ran around and popped open the hood of his antagonist. Then he got back into his own car and pulled off. Horns erupted everywhere as the guy had to climb out and shut his hood before driving away, and as Stony noticed, by now the light had changed. That was worth a chuckle or two, and, he felt a hell of a lot better.

JJ helped him divide the five million in two, putting half in each suitcase and they left for the airport at 2 PM. It would take almost an hour to get there. JJ drove and skirted most of the afternoon traffic by taking Wireless Road over to Petchburi, "the strip," which was a wide street lined with bars, cheap hotels, souvenir and jewelry stores, virtually a 24-hour sin-city for the R&R crowd. The scorching tropical sun turned the crowded streets into a shimmering mass of dusty humanity. As luck would have it, JJ's air-conditioner was on the fritz. Around the Victory Monument and out of town to Don Maung International, Bangkok's airport.

Off to the side, away from the main terminal, was the Air America hanger. Air America was the CIA owned airline for Southeast Asia. They boarded a gleaming silver DC-3, whose engines were already warming, to be greeted by Stony's neighbor, Andy Glass, their pilot. Receding blonde hair, tripwire thin, he was one of the best. Admitting to only a nodding acquaintance elsewhere, within the embassy and here in the plane they could enjoy a casual friendship.

"You know, Andy, I've flown in quite a few planes these past few years, but this old DC-3 is the only one that gives me any sense of security," said Stony as they shook hands.

"She ain't fast, but she's built like a rock," answered Andy.

"Let's hope she don't fly like one," chided JJ.

Andy flipped the latches on an ice chest and pulled out three Singha beers. "Bar's open. Might as well go first class."

The plane was rigged for both passengers and cargo with only three rows of seats up front, the rest was open space with a small kitchenette and a toilet cubicle on opposite sides towards the back. The cockpit was open to the rest of the plane. They discussed the evening's plans. The flight would take about an hour or so, the delivery at least two. Andy and his co-pilot would wait at the Chiang Mai airport and fly them back. Stony speculated to JJ about Ba Maung's trip up there. It added an extra reason for caution.

"If any word has gotten out through the Chinats about the money, it could be Dodge City up there tonight," said Stony.

They lifted off and headed north before 4 pm. The flight generally followed the Chao Phraya River and its many tributaries north to slightly northwest up the middle of Thailand's central plain. Stony took a window seat on the east side of the plane, JJ on the west. JJ soon pulled his shade down in defense of the glaring sun. While JJ caught a catnap, Stony again enjoyed the view. Although they flew higher than the chopper of the other day, there was still much to see. They quickly passed over the ancient city of Ayutthaya, then over the great Chainat Dam with its still growing lake behind it. There was a great deal of water traffic. The light green and browns of the farms and rice paddies contrasted with the deep green of the jungle, which in turn was cut by the brownish green of the many waterways. The land below was very flat until it disappeared into the distant haze-shrouded low hills of the Khorat Plateau off to the east towards Cambodia and then Laos. Slowly the land developed into foothills which grew into northern mountains. Here the great teak forests began and the air would cool noticeably. They were approaching their destination.

Chiang Mai is Thailand's second city, with a population of about seventy thousand located in the mountainous area of northern Thailand. It is noted for its fine climate, scenery, elephants, roses and light-skinned beautiful girls. It even has a small resident expatriate population, many of whom are

Americans. Founded in 1296, it was the capital for over five-hundred years of the independent Lanna-Thai Kingdom, which holds the same beloved place in Thai hearts as the fabled Camelot does in the west. The center of town is still surrounded by the old moat. Chiang Mai has that special ambiance of a tropical, mountain city.

There are several ancient Buddhist temples, called wats, one built during the founding of the city, almost seven hundred years ago. Colorful people from various hill tribes are often in town, especially at the night markets, where they sell handicrafts.

The flight became rough, mostly due to the low altitude, so the offer of a second beer was politely refused. They landed at Chiang Mai's airport just after five. Several taxis were waiting outside and one of the drivers approached. Stony bargained him down from 50 baht to 30, thinking it ironic that he was carrying two and a half million dollars in his suitcase and he had just haggled to save a buck on a taxi.

As they headed north on the narrow jungle-crowded road, Stony asked, in broken English, if the driver was willing to drive them to the village of Chom Thong. Without hesitation, he agreed.

"More 50 baht."

"40."

"OK"

The village of Chom Thong was between Chiang Mai and the highest peak in Thailand, Mount Inthanon, about 8400 feet at the summit. The Chinats had refused to make the deal in Chiang Mai, probably wanting to avoid the Thai authorities, and had wanted the delivery to take place in the near-border town of Mae Hong Son, about another five hour drive. As a compromise, and to maintain his position of independence, Stony agreed to the little mountain village of Chom Thong.

Meanwhile they had another little problem to deal with.

CHAPTER 5

Suddenly another Toyota taxi, coming from the opposite direction bore down on them. Just in time their driver swerved off the road, raced a short distance down a narrow lane and slammed on his brakes in a small clearing. The light was poor as Stony and JJ strained to see into the brush. Three mountain tribesmen, armed with primitive crossbows, sprang from the underbrush. Small, thin men, barefooted, each had a rag tied around their bushy, coal-black hair, wearing unbuttoned, light-colored shirts above short skirts or paisans. Despite their small size, they were a fierce looking group. They yelled something in Thai. The driver jumped from the taxi, hands in the air, motioning for Stony and JJ to do the same.

"Dodge City, Stony, just like you said," mumbled JJ as he reached for his 45 automatic.

"Just a minute, JJ," whispered Stony, "something about those guys. They look more scared than mean. They're looking at us like we were cobras. Something else is going on here. Let's cooperate while we try to figure this out." JJ didn't argue but he didn't look too happy about things either.

They eased out of the cab, leaving the suitcases inside. The cabby and a tribesman were evidently arguing about something. Audaciously, JJ pointed to one of the crossbows and, in pigeon English and sign language, asked how much the crossbow cost in Thai baht. The weapons were pretty primitive looking, but they could undoubtedly do their job. The native grinned a mostly toothless grin from a red betel-nut stained mouth and offered his crossbow. JJ smiled, slowly pulled out his wallet and held out a 100 baht note. The exchange was made. Over the driver's obvious objections, the other two offered their weapons. JJ bought them also. Curiously, the driver kept his hands in the air. Stony figured since things weren't going according to plan, he was still trying to play both sides. The tribesmen gleefully bounded into the underbrush and the driver hurriedly urged his passengers to mount up and get out of there.

Before they reached the main road, JJ, sitting behind the driver slid his 45 automatic over the top seat and into the neck of the driver.

"We go Chom Thong, you little bandit. CHOM THONG!"

"Chom Thong, OK! OK! Chom Thong!" the driver nervously shouted.

They careened down the darkening airport road into Chiang Mai and followed the ancient moat that surrounds the inner city to the Suan Dawk gate, turned left past the Buddhist temple of the same name and threaded their way out of town. It was very dark now. Once they were well down the road, JJ motioned the driver to slow down, and then directed him to turn down a nearby narrow lane. A hundred feet off the road he reached over and shut off the motor, then jumped out, opened the driver's door and yanked him out. He threw him face down over the hood. He quickly frisked him, throwing into the brush a small pocket knife. He spun the driver around and shoved his gun deep into his neck.

"TALK, you scumbag, TALK!" growled JJ.

Stony killed the headlights, leaving the parking lights as the only illumination in the otherwise pitch blackness. The petrified driver began spilling out broken English.

"Man pay me 200 baht. Say take you Chaing Mai."

"Who? I want a name! Who?"

"No name! Me don't know name. Just man. He pay me, I do."

"You lying little bastard. You didn't take us to Chaing Mai; you drove us into an ambush. TALK TO ME!" JJ jammed his .45 deeper into the driver's neck.

"OK! OK! 200 baht. Meo…Meo want suitcase. He pay Meo 50 baht for suitcase. That all! That all! No hurt you – I promise – no hurt you."

"Man. Was he a white man? American?"

"No."

"Burmese, maybe?"

"No. Thai. He Thai man. He pay Meo for suitcase."

JJ turned to Stony, "That's bullshit! They ignored the suitcases. This could only have been a hit. Maybe your Burmese guy. Any case, this little bastard knows more than he's telling."

"That's probably why they dumped those two-dollar crossbows for a profit and split. They more than doubled their money and didn't have to do something they didn't want to do anyway. I had a gut feeling this just didn't look like a robbery. What are we going to do with him?" asked Stony, motioning towards the driver.

The driver answered that question himself. Seeing JJ distracted by conversation, he took his chance. He made a grab for the gun. It was no contest. Instantly, JJ pulled the trigger. The bullet tore upward through the top of the driver's head, splattering blood. JJ grabbed two handfuls of clothing and threw him deep into the jungle underbrush. With no discussion, they got into the taxi, JJ driving, and headed up the road to Chom Thong.

Eventually, JJ spoke. "Cost me fifteen bucks back there to save your skin, ol' buddy."

"Seven-fifty, ol' buddy. Seems to me your neck was in that noose too. And you didn't even keep your souvenirs. Hell, we probably could have sold them to Pete and John and doubled our money."

"You mean, my money," he grinned. They continued on in silence.

Eventually they entered the village where only a few dim streetlights timidly relieved the enveloping blackness. It was quiet; almost no one was on the streets. Shops were closed, faint bare-bulb light filtered from shut tight houses. They passed by the Buddhist temple and noticed up ahead that one storefront seemed to be open. It must be the restaurant.

"Rolled up the sidewalks pretty early tonight. Probably means our friends are here as unwelcomed guests," mentioned Stony.

The designated meeting place was to be a restaurant just down the road from Wat Phra Tat Si, a famous old Buddhist temple. Evidently the open storefront was it. They drove past the obvious destination, nosed the taxi to the side of the road in a very dark spot, grabbed the suitcases and walked back to the restaurant. It was small and dimly lit. They took a table in a corner. The only other customer was sitting near the door at a table with a bottle of Mekong Whiskey on it. He left and returned with three friends, none of whom Stony recognized, although they were all Chinese. He noticed they each were armed, he figured with American supplied 45's. An elderly Thai lady, probably the owner, sat in silence in the back, offering no services.

"Dodge City?" inquired JJ. Stony didn't reply, he just nodded as he reached under his shirt and eased the 38 into his lap, absently tapping the suitcase with the toe of his boot.

"There is no need for that, my friend." The speaker stepped from the dark into the restaurant. The four Chinese quickly stood up. He motioned for them to sit. They did. He approached Stony and JJ with a smile. They stood and Stony extended his hand.

"Chan Li, we meet again." They all shook hands and sat down. The little old lady approached, hands pressed flat together as in prayer, she bowed in the traditional Thai greeting. They had a couple of beers while discussing the Chinats obligations as spelled out by a separate military briefing team that had visited here three days ago.

As they got up to leave, Chan Li chided Stony, "Well, my cowboy friend, I can tell you that all simulations will be in place in five days and we will pretend to be a major force attacking the communist dogs from the rear. It will not work, but we will have been paid handsomely for our efforts. Would you care to come along?"

"Sorry, got other irons in the fire," answered Stony.

"Then we will not keep you." He leaned close to Stony, "Say hello to John Wayne for me." Then in a more serious tone, "You had some trouble before?"

"A little. How'd you…never mind. Good luck."

The money had not been mentioned; they simply left the suitcases by their chairs. The taxi had been conveniently re-parked out front, motor running. JJ drove.

It was a quiet ride down the ink-black mountain road back to the Chiang Mai airport, each man involved in his own thoughts. Stony reflected on what a brutal and turbulent world he had stepped into. As an ordinary civilian back in Colorado, he had no idea. All of Southeast Asia had become the OK Corral. The Vietnam War was raging only a 45 minute flight away and all the neighboring countries were caught up in the maelstrom as major and minor nations battled each other in the ruthless pursuit of national goals. Under the shadowy shroud of espionage existed a netherworld of unconstrained violence. 'And this ol' cowboy is ridin' a hurricane horse to hell.'

"Not if I can help it," he absently said out loud. JJ glanced over and continued driving.

To break the monotony, Stony asked, "How'd you get into this line of work, JJ?"

"In a roundabout way, I suppose, Stony. Went to Marquette University on a football scholarship. It paid for schooling but not much else. One night I was in an Italian pizza parlor that had a piano. Being bored, I went over and played a couple of tunes. Can't read a note, but I can repeat almost any tune by ear. Funny how a little ten foot walk can change your life. The owner put a mug of beer on top of the piano – as long as I played, he supplied the beer. Seemed like a sweet deal to me. But after a couple of months of this my grades nose-dived and they kicked me off the team. I was too embarrassed to go home, so I joined the Army. They put me into the intelligence field. Found it fascinating. When I got out, I completed college on the GI Bill and applied to the Agency. Been there ever since. That's the story."

"Short and sweet. Just the facts Ma'am," Stony chided. "Now that you've opened yourself up so well, I've got another question, that is, if you feel like answering it."

"Shoot."

"I'm just curious about why, given the chance, you always do the driving?"

"Okay. I'll answer that one too. Believe me, it ain't nothing against you. About five years ago we were riding with a guy on a rainy night, coming out of DC heading west. Me, Ruthie and him, all in the front seat, kids in the back seat. Some jerk cuts us off and this guy panics. He locks the wheels and we rammed into oncoming traffic, head on. Me and the guy got pretty banged up, my oldest girl got a broken leg out of it, but I almost lost Ruthie. Touch and go for several days. It was a real bad time. I knew in my heart that if I had been driving, it never would have happened. For a couple of years I wouldn't ride with anybody – always drove." He paused. "Now it's just habit, I guess." He glanced over at Stony, "Wanna drive?"

The pilot was pacing around the plane when they arrived. JJ parked the taxi off to the side in a darkened area. As they stepped out of the dark the pilot jumped.

"Jeez, you guys had me worried. Run into trouble?"

"Nothing much. Let's get the hell out of Dodge," answered JJ.

That night, after stopping by the embassy to drop of his weekly letter to the kids, he headed for his rendezvous with the guys. He wasn't all that enthusiastic about boys' night out; in fact while his wife had been there, he'd rarely gone. He left his car in the parking lot of the Embassy and took a taxi to the bar. He never knew what these nights could lead to and when he drank too much he tended to forget that the Thais drive on the left-hand side of the road. He remembered the last boys' night out several months ago when they had gone bar-hopping. Sometime during the night, they had the good sense to park the cars and all take a taxi. Unfortunately, the next day, no one could remember just where, in a city of several million people, they had left the cars. It took them four hours to find them. Of course, by that time, they probably shouldn't have driven them home.

It was just after nine when he stepped into the Blue Lantern bar on Petchburi Road, after threading his way through a small crowd of pimps, whores and taxi drivers on the Strip. Some were eating one of their many small meals of the day from a food cart loaded with various dishes and hot spices and hung with dried fish and octopus. He could never get used to the pungent odor of octopus. He stopped just inside the door and peered into the dimly lit room. Typical R&R bar with loud music, walls lined with plastic covered booths, a few center tables, two couples swaying on the small dance floor, the smell of cheap perfume, old cigarettes, and stale beer.

"Over here Stony," yelled Pete above the din of the small band, "we'd about given up on you."

"Stop off for a little, ol' buddy?" chuckled John.

"Now you know better than that," quipped Pete, "Ol' Stony ain't dipped his wick in nothin' local since he's been here."

"Where's Allan, didn't he show?" asked Stony as he slid into the big corner booth next to JJ, and hoping to change the subject.

"He's in the can. Been there awhile. I better go check." said John. He was back in a flash, a mischievous grin on his face.

"Allan's taking a crap," he laughed, "pants down around his ankles and all. Pete, you go tell those other tables we're just pulling a prank." He winked at Stony and JJ. Everybody knew how panicky Allan could be. John waited a few seconds, eased into the men's room, put a match to a couple of paper towels and dropped them into the sink. He eased out, waited a few more seconds, and then threw the door open screaming, "FIRE! FIRE! EVERYBODY OUT!"

And he stepped back.

The men's room door bust open, out dashed Allan, naked from the waist down, his pants flying around one ankle as he raced madly for the door. John staggered back to the booth, doubled over with laughter, as was everyone else. Gasping as he tried to talk he chortled, "Bet he's out there trying to get them pants untangled with those taxi drivers, GI's and whores all staring at him!" A new burst of laughter all around.

"You're going to pay for this one, John boy," laughed JJ.

Suddenly the front door flew open, Allan came running in and dived under the big round table, scrambling to the rear. "Quiet! Don't say a word," he whispered loudly. Just then two MP's walked in, peering searchingly around in the darkness.

"You guys looking for that maniac that just run in here?" yelled John.

The MP's turned towards the group. Stony heard Allan whimper.

"He ran around the bar and out that back door over there." He pointed the way. The MP's hurried out, on the chase.

Pete gave everyone a big wink, "Better squat there awhile Allan, in case they come back." He passed a beer under the table. They all did their best to choke back the laughter, with little success.

"Yep," thought Stony, "another typical night out with the boys."

It went on like that for hours. John finally convinced Allan that saving him from the MP's ought to make up for that little joke between friends. Things broke up around 2 AM. As Stony was about to hail a cab, JJ took his arm.

"How about a nightcap. There's a guy I want to talk to. He may know something." They hailed a taxi and directed it down Petchburi Road, left on Rajdamri, and right on Rama, past the Intercon. Around the next traffic circle, they pulled up to an abandoned hotel. Stony noticed another taxi had pulled up just down the street. Nobody got out.

"There used to be an open-air rooftop restaurant on the fifth floor. Now they just use the inside bar," said JJ. "There's another bar somewhere downstairs. Never been to it. This guy's name is Big Jim, big black guy. He's one of those foreign managers. Did something in Rangoon before coming here."

There were a number of these personable foreigners, "fahrangs" in Thai, who fronted for locals as bar managers. They created a following and evidently were good for business. The elevator worked and they were soon stepping into a small adequately lit lounge. From a Hi-Fi came background jazz.

A large black man strode forward, "Evening gentlemen, how about a table?"

They ordered beers which were brought by a scantily clad waitress. JJ motioned for the greeter and he came over and took a chair.

"What can I do for you fellows?" asked Big Jim.

"This is my friend Stony and he needs some information on that Burmese gentleman you and I discussed yesterday," said JJ.

Big Jim scowled, "I'm not in the information business, sir. That's how I survive in my chosen profession," he started to get up.

JJ grabbed his wrist, squeezing hard. Big Jim's eyes fixed him in a vicious glare.

"This guy's wife was killed here not long ago and your Burmese may have been part of it. We *need* the information." JJ glared back.

Big Jim jerked free. He leaned close to them, "Alright, I can only tell you this, and then I'll deny it came from me. He is not in the Ex-Im business. That is not his wife he is with, and I'm told, he can be very dangerous. He's here for some specific reason, I know that." And he was gone.

"Sorry, Stony. Not much new, I'm afraid. Thought we'd get more out of him."

"I don't know, JJ, he may just have told us more than he realized."

While they were talking to Big Jim, a young Thai man, early twenties, had stepped into the lounge. He had taken a stool at the bar and was now walking slowly towards the men's room behind Stony. Suddenly, JJ threw his beer mug at Stony, narrowly missing the top of his head. It caught the Thai man in the chest, splashing beer up into his face. He stumbled back, dropping an open switchblade. He darted for the emergency exit, hitting the door so hard that when it opened he sprawled face-forward onto the floor outside. He scrambled to his feet as the door began to shut.

"Where does that go?" shouted JJ to Big Jim.

"Out to the old rooftop restaurant, but don't worry, he can't open it to get back in here," shot back Big Jim.

"Get back in? Hell I'm worried he'll get away," answered Stony and he and JJ ran for the door. Guns drawn, they kicked open the door and ducked back. Silence.

"There's a circular fire-escape over to the far left, behind the stage," offered Big Jim.

At the ready, they semi-crawled to some stacked tables, working their way towards the stage. They heard their man, in the back to the far right, evidently trying to find an exit.

"Sorry for almost hitting you with my mug, Stony, but when I saw the flash of that knife, I just reacted," whispered JJ.

"I think I figured that out almost as fast as you threw. Thanks to you, my throat's still intact. What the hell are you doing?"

"Taking a whiz. Too much beer tonight," answered JJ as he watered down the wall behind an old upright piano.

Just then the punk streaked past them on the balcony outside and raced down the fire-escape. Stony leaped through the open window and lunged down the stairs after him, JJ close behind. It was a circular five floors with Stony alternately leaping steps and hand sliding on the rail when he could. The adrenaline was pumping from both anger and action. The punk found his pistol and fired blindly upwards twice as he fled. At the bottom, out of breath, Stony had almost caught him, but ducked as the punk fired again backwards and hit a support column close to Stony's head. He felt the stinging impact of splattered concrete on his temple. The punk was getting away, running along the still full hotel swimming pool. Stony grabbed a deck chair and flung it with all his might. It hit the punk, knocking him into the pool. Stony dove in after him, grabbing him from the rear with one arm around the throat while trying to get control of his gun with the other. They went down once, twice, Stony couldn't get enough air. He squeezed the guy's throat so hard he thought he would snap his head; still he hung onto the gun. Finally the punk went limp, the gun dropping to the bottom of the pool. He let go. JJ helped him up and out of the pool, handing him back the 38 and his wallet he had thrown down as he dove in. He sat there a moment or two, catching his breath.

"We'd better get out of here," said JJ.

Down a few steps, they opened a door to a hallway. The other bar was on their right. Since Stony was dripping wet they figured to hole up here until he had dried some and not be so noticeable. It was a very small place, not thirty feet square, with a three-piece band blaring rock-n-roll so loudly no conversation was possible. It was packed with partiers, most dancing drunkenly. They sat at a tiny table and JJ held up two fingers to the waitress. It was almost 4:00 A.M. JJ leaned back to draw on his beer and stared. Stony caught the look and turned to follow the stare.

Behind him the wall was almost all glass. Several large windows looked underwater into the unlit pool. They could barely make out the punk floating face down. JJ put some money under his bottle and they eased out and headed for the street. They walked a few blocks while they discussed the hit man and Stony dried out. Later they found out the pool was sometimes used for an underwater strip-tease act for the bar patrons.

"Been a hell of a night, Stony. You know, hanging around you is getting to be dangerous, but damn it sure ain't boring."

"What can I say, JJ? I sure wouldn't be offended if you wanted to put a little distance between us."

"Are you kidding? This is the most fun I've had since I've been in this hellhole."

Hellhole? Why some people consider this a pleasure paradise."

"Trying to stay away from the pleasures is what makes it hell."

"That's the price of integrity, JJ. Just the price for integrity. I'm sure your wife appreciates it, even if she doesn't know about it. What say we head over to Pat Pong for a nightcap and then grab some breakfast?"

They had walked a few blocks and Stony felt dry enough not to attract much attention. They hailed a cab.

The taxi dropped them off at the Horseshoe Bar, famous in Bangkok for its semi-circular bar with mostly nude dancing girls on a stage in its center. Pat Pong was sort of downtown and was frequented mostly by foreigners in town for the long term. They didn't seem to own alternate, 'throwaway' bars so several of them took a chance and stayed open into the wee hours. They had a beer and JJ made another trip to the men's room. When he returned he grabbed Stony's arm and led him towards the rear of the bar. He stopped, put up a cautionary arm and pointed to a couple heavily intertwined in a booth. It was Allan and a street girl. Without a word, they returned to their beers at the bar.

"Maybe we ought to hose them down," grinned Stony, "they're going to start steaming the place up any minute."

"It ain't the first time. Bet you didn't know he spends a fortune on hookers."

"Probably because the word is out with all the round-eyes that he's a lecher," answered Stony. "Word is, he's hit on every woman in the embassy. Come on, I'll buy you breakfast at the Imperial's coffee shop."

JJ grinned mischievously and motioned for the bartender. He led him to the far end of the bar and pointed out Allan and his partner. He handed the bartender a 50 baht note and told him to send a round of drinks to his friend and his girl.

"No," the bartender replied.

"Whadya mean no?" huffed JJ.

"No girl. Kitoy."

"Kitoy! You gotta be kidding. Are you sure?" asked a stunned JJ.

"Me sure. I know this man. He bring same kitoy here before, many time."

JJ turned a definite pale. "Stony, I mean, I think he's a piece of crap, but this. There must be some mistake. Let's get out of here." They hailed a taxi and headed for the Imperial coffee shop.

Over a breakfast of hamburger steak and eggs, Stony's favorite when he couldn't get his Huevos rancheros, they discussed the situation. It was possible, no; it must be probable that Allan didn't know he was with a kitoy. It seemed strange to Stony that in a land of beautiful women, some fine looking women were really female impersonators

— kitoys. It was kinda crazy to think Allan had been all wrapped up with another guy.

"Hope you have some money left, Stony, that bartender kept mine," said JJ as they finished their coffee. "Sure went through a lot of money tonight. Ought to go back and claim my fifty."

"When that bartender said no, he meant no girl. He probably still sent those drinks. And that means Allan is probably in a sweat wondering who saw him and sent those drinks to boot."

"Serves the lowlife right. You know, Stony, you could use this to get him out of here and off your back. Think about it."

"I've been thinking about it, JJ. But not yet. If I was wrong, I'd be hurting someone who was once sort of a friend. We'll see. Time for some shut-eye."

They hoofed it to the embassy, picked up their cars and headed home.

The much needed sleep was not to be. At 9 A.M. the phone rang. It was Allan, not sounding all that awake himself. He wanted Stony to meet him at the embassy ASAP. He couldn't say why, just to hurry. Stony protested that it was a Saturday morning, but it did no good. So after a quick shave and shower, he headed down to the embassy. At this late hour of the morning, traffic was terrible. There are no weekends in the Orient.

Since he had no air-conditioning in the replacement for the 67' Dodge, Stony always tried to find his usual shady spot under a tree. The tropical sun could melt plastic seats, and his were black plastic to boot. As he strolled towards the front door of the embassy, he noticed Allan parking also. A woman driving an older dark gray Buick pulled in next to him and in getting out, she had hit Allan's car with her door. She was walking away when Allan jumped out and shouted,

"Hey lady. Get back here at once."

She turned, obviously startled, "Are you speaking to me?"

"I certainly am. If you don't return here at once, I will call security and inform them that you left the scene of an accident." He reached in his pocket, pulled out a cigarette and lit it with a match.

"Are you crazy? What on earth are you talking about?" The lady was incredulous.

"You just hit my car with your car." Allan was shouting. "That constitutes an automobile accident."

"Sir, I merely bumped your car with my door." She was coming back to the 'scene'.

"You nicked my paint. You damaged my car. That's no small thing. Now it will rust, it might spread." He was very agitated. "This is the tropics lady, if you give rust a chance, it will take over. My paint job is ruined now. I may even have to take this car to a body shop."

"And just what do you propose we do?" The lady was becoming irritated. She clutched her small purse up to her shoulder, almost like a weapon. A nice looking woman, one of the older secretaries, probably late forties, slim, with short gray hair.

"I propose we exchange insurance information."

"Are you serious?"

"Very serious."

The lady hesitated. Finally she relented. "Oh, all right, but I am in a hurry, could we do this quickly? I have just been called in to replace the on-duty staff secretary and I am somewhat late as it is."

Stony leaned against his car, observing all this. The woman glanced his way, plaintively once, Allan didn't. As the woman hurried away, Allan walked over to Stony. He was already sweating in the morning air, looking very hung-over. He hadn't gotten much sleep either.

"You really intend to pursue that, Allan?"

"Probably not. No. Just wanted to give that thoughtless broad a hard time. People that do that really tick me off. I'll bet the next time she throws her door open, she'll be a lot more careful."

As they turned to walk towards the embassy, Allan stopped and turned to look at Stony. He stared into his face for a long moment, as if trying to read something there.

"You all right Allan?"

"Yea. Yea. I'm fine, little hung over, but I'm fine. The ambassador wants to see me right away. Said to bring along a good man, I guess that's you. Let's go." He lit a cigarette.

"How about some coffee first." It wasn't a question. As they walked through the entrance doors, Stony caught sight of the ambassador's car entering the grounds. He said nothing to Allan, even with his poor company; coffee was more important right now. As they signed in with the Marine Security Guard, Stony asked, "Any fresh coffee back there, Bill?"

Bill grinned, "Sure is, made fresh only about two hours ago."

"Ought to put you on every Saturday, usually it's only six hours fresh."

Since their own office hadn't opened up yet and the snack bar was closed for the weekend, Stony led the way back to the Marine Security Guard office and poured them both paper cups of coffee, and handed one to Allan.

"The ambassador give you any idea why he had to see you so early on a Saturday morning?"

"No, only that it was important. When the ambassador summons you, you don't ask questions, you just go."

They finished their coffee and climbed the stairs to the second floor office of the ambassador.

CHAPTER 6

The ambassador, casually dressed this morning in a light tan Madras shirt and slacks that belied his serious demeanor, offered chairs. No small talk, he got right to the point.

"Mister Huehner, Mister McGraw, I apologize for asking you here on a Saturday morning, and I realize you presently have your hands full, but it appears that we are in need of your unique services. What I am about to divulge must be kept in the strictest confidence." They nodded their ascent.

"I had a visit from a Chinese gentleman last night. He was very concerned about a rather nasty problem that has reared its head here in Bangkok recently. The resolution of this is of the greatest importance to this gentleman, to the American government, and to our friends, the Thai government. It is also a very ticklish situation for me as an official representative of the Unites States."

"Why don't you just spell it out sir," said Stony, impatiently risking impertinence.

"All right, Mister McGraw. The situation is this. You are probably aware that the Chinese underworld controls the prostitution and owns most of the R&R bars here in Bangkok. You are also probably aware that two young soldiers have been killed in separate incidents but under mysterious circumstances recently."

"We are aware of those things, yes sir," answered Allan.

The ambassador was definitely uncomfortable.

"Then you would understand that if another soldier or two were to be killed here, it could seriously jeopardize Bangkok as an R&R destination, with the attendant loss of revenue that could very seriously undermine relations between this country and ours, at a critical juncture in our pursuit of the Vietnam situation."

"Not to mention the serious loss of revenue to the Chinese gentleman and his friends," interrupted Stony, which elicited a hard stare from the ambassador.

"Not very diplomatic, Mister McGraw, but to the point, nevertheless. Now this fellow, last night, offered what I think is a workable solution, if pursued with the utmost discretion. That's where your office comes in, Mister Huehner. The Chinese would like to establish a liaison, between one of their members and one of ours. Their member would inform our man where the young man in potential trouble could be located and our man would go to the location and pick him up, so to speak. In other words, we would remove him from harm's way and thereby avoid a potentially nasty situation. I'm sure you understand that the United States government could, in no way, be perceived as having dealings on an unofficial level with an underworld organization."

"We understand completely, sir. I'll have Mister McGraw here get on this immediately," said Allan, without looking at Stony.

Stony knew the drill. One more obstacle. One more effort to get him to go home.

"What's the next step, sir?" he asked.

"It seems like they like to do business in some after hours club known as the Barge. Do you know of this place?"

"I know of it."

"In that case, you are to ask the doorman for a Mister Joey Li. I must warn you, Mister McGraw, you will be pretty much on your own with this. We can acknowledge nothing," reiterated the ambassador.

"I'm no stranger to working like that, sir," said Stony, "and I am familiar with Mister Li."

"Then I leave the details up to you, sir. Keep me informed, especially of any problems. Good luck."

Stony couldn't help but wonder if the ambassador's constricted vernacular developed on the job, or did it help him to get the job. It always sounded more like a press release than a conversation.

Back in the office, Stony pulled what info he could on the local underworld. It wasn't much. He opened a file, stared at it and began to think this thing through. The Chinese were the largest minority within Thailand, comprising about three million of the twenty-six million people. As they do in many Oriental countries, they control most of the local underworld, reaping the lion's share of the rewards from these enterprises. Although prostitution wasn't illegal in Bangkok, it was lucrative, especially during the Vietnam era, and so they controlled most of this also. But the control isn't total, since some of the young pimps are hotshots, under the illusion that they are warlords of a sort themselves.

The situation, as Stony saw it was this: A young GI comes to Bangkok for four days of Rest and Recuperation – R&R, from the terror of war in the jungles of South Vietnam. As he leaves the mandatory military briefing upon arrival, there is, lined up along the curb, a taxi, a driver, and a girl, offered as a package, 24 hours a day, for his four day stay, for as little as a couple of hundred bucks. Many of the younger guys, not knowing any better, buy the package. It's not all that bad a deal for some. They visit a few souvenir shops and jewelry stores, steered by the driver, for a cut, and spend the rest of the time in bars or in the rack. For some it's four days of heaven after six months of hell. The trouble comes when the GI decides not to go back just yet. Now he's AWOL. In his sober moments he begins to get scared. He holds onto the girl; she's the only one he knows in this big strange city. Then he runs out of money. The girl is a money machine for the pimp. As soon as the GI is broke, he becomes a liability. Life is cheap in the orient, very cheap. Being a liability, he just may be killed to free up the girl.

After two of these incidents, the local underworld is looking for help before they lose a very lucrative business. Stony has become the solution. He would meet their contact man and they would 'work things out.'

Enough of this. He was tired and hungry, so after grabbing a cheeseburger from the Imperial coffee shop, he headed home to resume his fitful sleep.

That night he arrived at the Barge after-hours club about one-thirty, not in a good mood. He had decided to try a Thai version of a Mexican restaurant. He was sorry. The taco's were tasteless, the only hot sauce they had was Tabasco, good stuff but it ain't picante, and when he had pointed out the huge rat scavenging under the barstools, the waiter said it was no big deal. He didn't stay for desert.

The Club Barge was on Soi 2, at the end of the long narrow street that usually flooded after a rain. Being an after-hours club, it didn't open until 1 A.M. Periodically the authorities decide to clean up the night life scene, especially during periods of martial law, and since the law says bars must close at 1 A.M., anyone caught open later during one of these purges can be closed down permanently. Some take the chance, especially the Pat Pong Street bars, but many legit bars also own another 'after hours' bar that becomes expendable, if necessary. The doorman, bouncer, just happened to be the same one that worked at the Derby Club. Imagine that. Stony knew him well, a good man. Stony asked to see Joey Li, who he knew was also the owner of the Derby. The doorman led him to a table and departed. This was a large nightclub, as they go, dimly lit and crowded with late night partiers, probably a couple hundred at least. The band was so loud that conversation was impossible. They were playing what seemed to be the theme song for the Bangkok bars at the time – "The Age of Aquarius." While the patrons writhed to the beat on the crowded dance floor, the ever present twirling and mirrored globe in the ceiling cast its bits of moving light around in its circular pattern.

Stony saw Joey, at a large corner booth, with several other men, each accompanied by a pretty young girl. Their eyes met, Joey smiled and nodded. A waitress brought a beer. He waited. Finally, the band took a break and not quite so loud recorded music filled the room. Joey Li slid into the chair next to Stony. Smiling broadly, he held out his hand. He was a good looking young Chinese man, probably no more than 25, sharply dressed. He came over to Stony's table alone, but Stony noticed his men in the booth never took their eyes off him.

"You have come about our situation?"

"I have."

They discussed several options and decided that whenever Joey needed him he would leave a message at Stony's office and they would meet at the Barge for particulars. Stony would then collect the GI, and escort him back into military custody. It all sounded deceptively simple. It just so happened that Joey had some information on one such soldier tonight. He gave it to Stony, writing the address in Thai on a scrap of a paper so the taxi driver could read it.

"There is also another one, but I do not know just where he is hiding at the moment. The information is supposed to be brought to me tonight. Would you care to wait?" Joey said in surprisingly proper English. This was a sharp young man who was going places in his profession.

"Tell you what, I'll try to round up this one and check back with you later tonight."

Outside, he left his car and grabbed a taxi, once inside, he handed him the address. Stony wasn't all that comfortable with this situation, but he had willingly taken the job because he reckoned that being killed in 'Nam was bad enough, but being killed for some pimp's cash flow shouldn't happen to any mother's son.

The cheap hotel was over in the Banglamphu section of Bangkok, north of Chinatown on a side street off Khao San Road. This area had long been a traveler's center, where the backpack trippers gathered in the cheap guesthouses, smoked their dope, obtained fake student ID cards, found places to wash their clothes and hung out temporarily while traveling Asia on the cheap.

Stony found the rundown, bare-bones hotel, and eased up to the third floor designated room. The door was unlocked, so pistol in hand, he cautiously opened it to find the GI alone, sound asleep. The girl had probably just recently slipped away. Stony shook the kid awake. Once he could converse, Stony laid out the facts. The kid seemed relieved in a way, still scared, but relieved. Stony escorted him to MACTHAI headquarters MP office and turned him over to the sergeant on duty. He taxied back to the barge.

As he threaded his way through the cars in the small crowded parking lot, a foreigner and his Thai girl were leaving. As he politely stepped between the cars to let them pass by, he smiled at the girl. The man had enough liquor in him to take offense at this and he turned and shoved Stony. The guy growled something in a Brit or Aussie accent, but before Stony made a move they were suddenly surrounded by several Thai's.

"Sir, if you would please to enter club, we handle this."

"Sure, no harm done." Stony was more amused than riled.

The other guy was being unceremoniously hustled into a taxi. As he entered the club, Joey Li waived him over. The music was still deafening. Joey handed him a note written in English with the wanted information on it about the other AWOL.

"Job's done. Thanks. Time for some shut-eye. I'll pick up this other maverick later," he said loudly into Joey's ear. It was almost 4 A.M.

Joey yelled back, "You talk funny, but I like you. We will work well together."

Just then the doorman came over and said something to Joey. He stiffened, and then leaned close to Stony, "My apologies. That man will never bother you again. No one makes trouble for our friends."

Stony looked questioningly at him. Joey drew his finger across his throat. He shook his head no to Joey, but Joey motioned it was too late to stop it. Life was so cheap here in the orient.

He had already decided that ethics prohibited his accepting anything other than food or drinks from these guys. It wasn't only his ethics, but those of the U.S. government. But it wasn't only ethics. He was aware that they liked to bestow sometimes elaborate gifts on business associates, not only as expressions of friendship but also to subtly put the person into a position of being beholden to them. Stony was not going to be indebted to these guys in any way, if he could help it. Besides, in a society that considered 'face' a critical social factor, he could only save 'face' by not accepting gifts at all. He would never lose his independence to this bunch. But how in hell was he going to handle this? They killed a guy just because he had hassled Stony. After some thought, he came to the conclusion that he hadn't asked for it, had even protested it, albeit too late. He regretted it but he refused to feel guilty over it.

The band took a break. Seeing the grim look on Stony's face, Joey smiled, clasped him on the shoulder and said, "I always like to eat after a long night. I insist you join us for breakfast."

It had been an eventful night, and he *was* hungry, so along with several of Joey's group, Stony piled into a white Mercedes out front of the club, which was followed by another with more of the group. They glided down Ploenchit Road in the direction of the Intercon, but turned left into one of the streets of Siam Square and stopped before a two-story Chinese restaurant. It had an opulent décor. Lavishly trimmed with black and deep red lacquer, the walls were covered in pale green Thai silk which held bright golden, long-tailed dragons. Even at this early morning hour it was crowded. Joey Li approached the Maitre D', said just a few words and the Maitre D' flew upstairs.

Joey turned to Stony, "It will only be a few moments."

With that it appeared as if a fire drill was being enacted as dozens of people quickly descended the wide circular staircase and disappeared out the restaurant doors. Moments later the Maitre D' appeared at the top of the stairway bowing and bidding them up. What had been an upstairs crowded with diners was now empty except for the waiters busily cleaning off tables. A U-shaped arrangement of tables had been made ready in the center of the room. They were graciously seated.

Stony mused to himself, "This is one powerful little Chinaman."

Joey motioned for him to sit in the empty chair next to him, and waiving his arm towards the rest of the room, "I like my privacy. The menu is only in Chinese, may I order for you?"

"I reckon in this case, it's the only way to go," Stony replied, "and this is a hell of an introduction to the Chinese Mafia." Uncharacteristically, he had spoken before he thought. "No offense intended."

"Chinese Mafia… Chinese Mafia. I'll remember that." He was beaming, said something in Chinese to the group, who seemed to think it was pretty funny. "Chinese Mafia…Stony, you are a pretty funny guy." He magnanimously offered Stony one of the girls, which Stony politely refused. The food was plentiful and as usual Stony ate what looked good and tasted good. The meal was accompanied by a strong Chinese wine that he didn't like so he drank the green tea.

Naturally everyone ate with chopsticks, which he had thankfully mastered long ago.

After breakfast he decided to pick up the other AWOL. Having been delivered back to the Barge and his car, he drove to Hualamphong railroad station and parked. He took a taxi again to the Banglamphu section of town. The little Toyota blitzed down the crowded, narrow side streets like a broken field runner. It slowed in front of the hotel, but Stony motioned him on down to the corner. He was wearing loose trousers and had his shirt outside, as usual, to hide his belt holster. He could feel the 22 in the special holster in his left boot. He walked back to the hotel, entered and climbed the stairs of the shabby, dimly lit building. On the second landing a heavy, surly Thai was guarding the door that Stony wanted. He nodded and started past him. He took the first stair, and then wheeled suddenly, kicking the man hard in the diaphragm. The man doubled over, gasping. Stony grabbed him and rammed his head into the stair post. He would be out for awhile. The loud music coming from inside was probably meant to cover up the pimp's rough-up of the girl or GI. That could work both ways. It didn't quite. Stony pulled his stubbed-nose 38 and braced himself against the wall. The door was slowly opening. A small pistol in a small hand protruded into the hallway. Stony came down hard on it with his own, the pistol clambered across the floor. When a head poked out looking for him, he kicked it hard. Two down. Spinning, Stony crossed the doorway, kicked it open and stepped in, gun pointing at the two men standing there. One had a pistol, haphazardly pointing in Stony's direction, evidently shocked into inaction.

"DROP IT!" he yelled.

Whether the man understood English or not, he dropped the gun. The other guy, obviously the big shot pimp, smirked. He was dressed better than the other three. Stony motioned them to one side of the room, including the one now sitting up on the floor, nursing an obviously broken hand and a rapidly swelling jaw. The girl was in a chair, her face bruised and swollen. The young, lanky GI, in his shorts, was standing wide-eyed in the corner.

"You okay, son?"

"Just scared, sir."

"Take the girl over there and sit on the bed." He turned to the pimp, "You speak English?"

"Yes. He speak it!" shouted the girl. The pimp glared.

Stony motioned to the girl, "That wasn't necessary."

The pimp just sneered and started towards the door. As he came near enough, Stony tripped him. When he started to get up, Stony punched him hard in the face. He went down.

"That was for the girl. I've always hated bullies. Now get out of here."

The timid gunman helped the pimp to his feet. Once up, the pimp roughly shoved him away and started for the door. Stony noticed him pulling a small caliber pistol out as they left. He kicked the door shut, just in time. It erupted in splinters as the pimp unloaded his pistol into it and then sprinted down the stairs. Nobody was hurt.

"Get dressed and let's get out of here."

He gave the GI the standard info. The kid seemed relieved. The girl took his hand and said very gravely, "Thank you." He gave her a hug.

Stony checked the hallway, then went to a front window and leaned out. He saw what he wanted. The little group of hoodlums had crossed the narrow street and were heading in the opposite direction Stony's trio would go. They had had enough, for now, at least.

They hailed a samlor at the door of the hotel. It wasn't as fast as a taxi, but it was all that could be had on these back alleys. At his car, Stony asked the girl if he could take her somewhere.

"No. I go home now. I be OK."

"What about the girl. What will happen to her?" asked the GI.

"She'll be alright. In a few days she'll be all healed up and back out on the streets. The pimp made his point. She's a money machine, she doesn't work, he's out the money. She got what she did because she stuck with you." He drove to the MP office at the MACTHAI compound, dropped off the GI and headed home for some much needed sleep.

Exhaustion allowed him to sleep until noon. He awoke hungry, so after a shower he descended to the first floor kitchen. The entire first floor of the house was one open room, a large living-dining room, with the kitchen in an alcove to the rear. Bare wood teak floors with large windows on three sides, which his wife had curtained to keep out the intense tropical heat. In one corner they had set up a bar for entertaining, which Stony never used anymore. He couldn't remember the last time he had sat in the padded rattan chairs that were almost the only other furnishings in the room. The house was just somewhere to clean up and sleep now. More depressing than inviting lately. He used to look forward to coming home to the wife and kids, not anymore.

Except for some beer, about the only thing he kept in the fridge were some cold cuts. He kept the bread in there also, to protect it from the invasive insects. Back home in Colorado the cold winters kept the insects in check, but here in the tropics it was a bug's paradise. He remembered his wife lining the cabinets with 'bug paper' and putting insect strips around all the doors and windows. She was always spraying. She waged constant war against the insect world, employing every little weapon available. Even let those little lizards, called geckos, co-exist with the family until she began to find too many 'droppings' and that offended her acute sense of cleanliness.

He layered two slices of bologna between a couple of slices of white bread, grabbed a beer and sat out on the verandah to eat. The maid's husband was squatting at the far corner. Wasn't much of a job for a man, gardening here, but it did keep them together. The yard didn't extend over ten feet on the front and to one side of the house. On the other two were the driveway and the maid's quarters. The yard was immaculate, he had to hand him that. The grass was carpet thick and cut neatly not over an inch tall. Various shrubs and flowers added to the color and there was a monster rubber tree over to one side. The only real detraction was that it was all surrounded by a six-foot chain link fence. Stony had also let them put up a small shrine to the 'house god' in the corner. They occasionally prayed there and burnt incense sticks.

A leaf fell from a shrub. The gardener walked over, picked it up and returned to his squat.

Stony smiled to himself. Wouldn't it be great if he had as good a handle on his job as this guy had on his? He finished the beer and returned inside.

Lousy lunch. There's nothing appealing about cold bread. On a whim he called Som-Marie. How about he pick her up early and they do some tourist stuff. She agreed.

Just before one o'clock he slowed in front of the pocket markets that line both sides of a canal off Sukhumvit Road and eased the car up to the flower stand he had used regularly up until a year ago. A dozen roses sold for 75 cents or 15 Thai baht, so he always gave the little old lady a twenty baht bill. At one time he had been such a regular that he could just slow down hold out the money and she would hand him the roses, always red. This time he came to a full stop. The same little old lady was there but she just stared at him. She knew. Everybody seemed to know. Just then she began to smile and came over carrying the roses.

Som-Marie was ready, another reason to like this girl. She thanked him for the roses, held them to her face, inhaling the aroma.

"My father used to bring my mother roses. You Americans are so romantic," she smiled, kissed him on the cheek and left the room to care for them. He thought she looked pretty sharp. A white headband set back in her flowing ebony hair, a white short sleeved blouse tucked into short navy blue culottes, great for touring. Even the little white tennis shoes looked cute on her. The whole effect gave her the look of a teenager, while showing off her beautiful figure.

When she returned she suggested it would be easier if they took taxi's today, so outside on the street they hailed a samlor – sort of a three-wheeled motor scooter with a small seat for two in back of the driver. They were a familiar sight on the back streets of Bangkok. It seemed there were thousands of them in the city. They function mainly as back street taxis. At Sukhumvit they left it and hailed a regular taxi.

"What would you like to see first, Mister Tourist?"

"I want to see it all. Let's start with the snake farm," he answered.

She directed the taxi driver to the Pasteur Institute, the snake farm's proper name. As they rode through the teeming, dusty streets, she slid her tender little hand into his.

"Your hands feel strong, muscular. They are not like any other man's hand I have touched," she said.

"Probably because you've known bureaucrats, you know, office hands. I come from a different background. My work has been mostly outside, building fence, loading hay, riding, roping, things like that. It's really the life I prefer and I hope to get back to it soon."

"I would love to see a real cowboy ranch. When I was younger I was in love with John Wayne. I went to all his movies that came to our little town of Hua Hin."

Stony looked deeply into her dark brown eyes, "I'd like that."

The taxi let them out at the main entrance to the Pasteur Institute. As they entered the park-like area, Stony noticed the lack of buildings to house the snakes. Instead, there were several large round pits, about fifty feet across and circled by a low stone wall. They seemed to be only about twelve feet deep. Inside the pits was a snake-haters nightmare. Each was teeming with dozens of snakes, the first with cobras, another with Russell's vipers. But the action was in a third pit, containing a dozen or so king cobras. A demonstration was about to begin. Into this pit slid five Thai men. Amazingly, most of these huge snakes ignored them. But several did not. They raised their heads, hoods spread, looking the men straight in the eye. The small crowd gasped, but the men went about their chore calm and determined.

Cobras can't leap but only fall forward, so one man acted as decoy to the chosen specimen, barely out of the snake's reach, while the others circled behind and wrestled it under control. The man kept a wary eye out for the others. Once the other four men had control of the beast, with great effort, the decoy quickly produced a membrane covered jar and forced it to the cobra's hissing mouth. As the fangs pierced the membrane, the liquid death flowed copiously. It was all the men could do to maintain control with the last man staggering under the power of the tail. Several other giant snakes were raised but kept enough distance that the work could continue. An assistant at the wall took the jar with a made to fit basket attached to a stick, and handed back a large pair of chopsticks and a cloth bag. The bag contained meat that was then force fed with the chopsticks into the snake's mouth. Cobras won't eat in captivity it seems, so they are kept alive by this method in order to continue to harvest the venom for research and anti-venom production.

Some present in the small crowd suddenly screamed as one of the giant snakes maneuvered behind one of the snake wrestlers, stalking him. The man barely escaped, leaping out of the way as it struck. He looked up at the crowd and shrugged it off, just a hazard of the job. On cue, they each released the writhing serpent and carefully but quickly exited the pit.

"Makes our little prairie rattlers seem downright friendly," remarked Stony.

They visited the python exhibit. Stony wasn't entirely at ease, so to make conversation, he related an incident to Som-Marie.

"You know, I almost ran over one of those once." They were watching the lethargic movement of the giant snakes. "One of the streets to our place is only one lane wide with a canal on one side with driveway bridges crossing the canal. One night my wife and I were coming home from a party, it was raining and visibility wasn't real good. I looked up the street to see if anyone was coming the other way, which meant one of us had to pull off into a driveway bridge to let the other pass. My wife screamed so I slammed on the brakes and backed up a little. In front of us was this python, maybe 10 to 12 inches thick, with its head going into the hedges on one side of the road and its tail still in the canal. It wasn't in any hurry, so we just waited. Next morning I told the gardener about it and he said it was no big deal; there was another one in the swampy lot down the street. I had often seen kids cooling water buffalo in that swamp and sleeping on their backs. Sometimes my wife and I walked down that street after a rain to watch the 'walking fish' run from puddle to puddle. But not after that."

She was smiling indulgently with that 'I've lived here a long time look'.

"Heard it a dozen times from us foreign types, huh? Well then, how about I buy us a drink at the Oriental?" After a brief tour of the rest of the grounds, they hailed a cab at the entrance.

The taxi careened kamikaze-like down Silom Road crowded with food pushcarts, bicycles, samlors, and orange-saffron robed monks with their shaved heads and bare feet, all somehow escaping this four-wheeled torpedo. The taxi dropped them off in front of one of the most beautiful old style hotels in the Far East., the historic Oriental Hotel. Situated serenely on the bank of the wide slow Chao Phraya

River, it exudes old world charm with its wide verandahs and overhead fans.

"Did you know this is one of the finest hotels in the whole world?" Som-Marie offered as they strolled slowly toward the lobby entrance, "They say it has a staff of three people for every room. Did you know it even has an 'author's wing' where suites are named for the famous authors who have stayed there?"

"Like who, for instance?"

"Like Somerset Maugham, oh, and Noel Coward, for instance. They just built that tower over there because of the demand for room, about ten years ago."

They happened onto an exotic Thai dance demonstration on one of the verandahs. The girls were finely costumed in rich, brightly colored satins with towering head ornaments. Their ballet-like movements were fluid and exact. Stony marveled at how they could bend their hands backwards so that their fingers touched their forearms. Afterward they slipped into the Oriental's Bamboo Bar. Som-Marie ordered two gin and tonics. It wasn't Stony's drink but it somehow seemed to fit.

"This place looks like a movie set, they could have filmed Casablanca right here." He sipped his drink. "What a contrast, we seem so far away from all the commotion of the rest of the city." He ordered another round and a light lunch.

Two neatly dressed Thai gentlemen walked past their table when one of them recognized Som-Marie. He stopped and spoke to her and then seemed to stare briefly but intently at Stony. As Stony watched they had an intense conversation for a couple of minutes and then the Thai gentlemen turned to Stony, nodded gravely and walked away.

"What was that all about?" he asked.

"The man I was talking to is named Lang Pibul. We went to college together and have been friends for many years. He works in what you would call the District Attorney's office as a senior police official. He wanted to know how long I had known you and said he recently had a tip that you should be a suspect in your wife's murder. He warned me that I might be in danger. He was very angry about the lack of cooperation from your embassy. Their investigation has gotten nowhere and because of the touchy diplomatic situation, he feels his hands are somewhat tied. He is very frustrated about it all."

"He can join the crowd." He finished his drink, "Well, I'm not going to let anything spoil such a beautiful day with such a beautiful girl, unless of course, you feel you are in danger."

She smiled, "Since you are enjoying yourself so well, I suggest we take a nice, slow, river taxi tour. You can relax while I point out the interesting sights."

They strolled slowly down to the Oriental's private pier and hired a river taxi. Som-Marie became the tour director. They boated over to Thonburi and visited the floating market, teeming with low canoe-like little sampans loaded to the limit with colorful upriver produce and just about anything else you could imagine. Most were staffed with women in bright colored blouses over body hugging sarongs, topped with conical wide-brimmed straw hats. A small boy swam up to their boat loaded down with brass temple bells. Stony was amazed at the weight he seemed to be carrying. He bought a couple of the bells, "Just to relieve him of some of the metal." Shanty like houses were built on stilts right out over the edge of the slow, muddy river with several wooden steps leading to the water. As they passed by the people carried on their normal business, oblivious to the river traffic. On one set of steps a woman was washing clothes; on another a boy was brushing his teeth, all in the filthy river water.

They cruised past the Temple of the Dawn, the Temple of the Reclining Buddha, the royal palace with its Temple of the Emerald Buddha, and on up to the royal barge sheds where they turned around for the return trip. All the while Som-Marie was explaining the sights. They had spent the afternoon touring and it was getting dark as they again passed the Temple of the Dawn. It was bathed in spotlights, highlighting an immense central pagoda, over 250 feet tall, decorated with thousands of bits of colored porcelain.

"Quite a site. A great ending for a great tour. I thank you. I'm hungry again. Know any good restaurants?" he grinned. Som-Marie directed the driver to a pier by the Memorial Bridge. They walked a few blocks through Chinatown and stopped in front of what appeared to be an ordinary office building.

"How about here?" She exhibited a mischievous grin.

Stony was puzzled but knew better than to underestimate this beautiful lady. They entered. Inside they slowly ascended three floors in a decrepit open cage elevator. Through an elaborately carved circular doorway, they entered another world.

It was only barely discernible that they were still inside a building. The roof was high above them, mostly glass with the supports barely visible. They found themselves on the edge of a stunningly attractive oriental garden with a narrow stream circling through and large carp gliding about in it. They were standing on a roofed-over, narrow porch that encircled three sides of the garden. Opening onto the porch were a continuous row of bamboo huts, open fronted, that served as dining niches. The crowning piece was a full grown ancient looking Banyan tree occupying much of the fourth wall with many aerial roots extending downwards six feet or so from a plethora of branches, giving the impression of a whole grove of trees.

Stony stared wide-eyed at all this, to the amusement of Som-Marie. Two Chinese ladies approached. One took their shoes while the other escorted them to their dining hut. Stony was still in awe as he adjusted his non-oriental legs under the low table.

"You said you liked Chinese. Do you like this?" asked Som-Marie.

"Yes. Yes! I'm amazed by it. That tree must have been there over fifty years!" he exclaimed. "My turn." He leaned over and kissed her on the cheek. "You are a fascinating lady. I'd like to know more about you."

"Like?"

"Well, for instance, we could start with your name. It is certainly unique," he suggested.

"Alright. I will tell you a little about myself, and then it is your turn."

"Fair enough."

"My mother taught at Chulalongkorn University, as I do, but she was a full professor, an 'acharn,' I am only an instructor. My father was an official in the American Consulate, in your embassy. They were very much in love. We lived here in Bangkok, of course, and I attended Ruam Rhudi School which is run by Catholic nuns. When I was ten years old my parents were killed in a plane crash on their way back from Vientiane. For awhile I went to live with my aunt in Hua Hin. It is a small town south of here on the west side of the Gulf of Thailand. It has an interesting geography and people. I lived there for seven years. Then a man from the Bangkok branch of the Bank of America found me and told me about a trust that had been set up by my parents through their will with some insurance. He said they had almost given up finding me. I returned to Bangkok and graduated from Thamasat University. Eventually I was hired as a Political Science instructor at Chula. Now your turn."

He looked at her thoughtfully for a moment, mentally digesting her story. He took another bite of who knows what – she had ordered – if it tasted good he ate it, and mostly it tasted good. It was amazing to him that she was still single. She was beautiful, intelligent, had a great personality. A certain sweetness, and a fine sense of humor. Was he…? Whoa! Slow down hoss. You got a history and she's got a history. Take things slow; don't let out your loop 'til you're sure you can hold on to what you catch.

"First a question. Have you ever been married? I mean, well, I'm sorry; you don't have to answer that. It's none of my business, but in America you would be every man's dream."

"Apparently not in Thailand. I doubt I am every man's dream, but it's really more complicated than that. I am the product of two cultures. I want an American style marriage, you know, fidelity to each other. Many Thai men believe there is nothing wrong in having a wife and a girlfriend. Also, I seem to intimidate some men. They don't like a girl with brains. And I have always avoided becoming involved with a foreign man, because I don't know if I could ever leave Thailand for long. I love my country, I am happy here. I go to the Derby Club because I like the international atmosphere and I sometimes meet interesting people. You,

Mister Stony McGraw, you scare me. I really like you and honestly I'm afraid of where this could lead."

Stony took a deep breath. She sure was straight forward, gotta give her that.

"Som-Marie, I was just thinking the same thing. But we've been given a gift here, you and me, and I, for one, don't want to lose what we've got. I say let's throw caution to the wind and ride this out, wherever it goes."

She threw her arms around him and kissed him on the mouth.

"Whew! That's some answer, Ma'am."

They just held each other for a while.

"Have you ever had plum wine?" she asked. He hadn't. They did, and it was very good, and over it he told her about himself, the kids, and the ranch, even how much he had loved his wife. Not maudlin, just the facts. As she listened attentively, he almost lost himself in her deep, dark, enchanting eyes. He had heard of shipboard romances and wondered of this would turn out to be like that – short and intense. He didn't want to think that way. It seemed dishonest, like getting married with a plan for the divorce. In his life right now he was ridin' a rough string and he was determined to give it an honest ride. He just hoped he could measure up.

He took her home and stayed the night with no regrets.

CHAPTER 7

As he pulled into the narrow street leading to his house, he noticed three cars already there; two patrol cars and one unmarked. The driveway gate was already open. As he pulled into the carport, he could see through the glass entry doors a small crowd of police in his living room. There were six khaki-uniformed officers and one plainclothesman. Maybe they had found something. Just in case, he slipped his 38 up under the driver's seat and wedged it between the side springs. Then he strolled nonchalantly into the house. The maid was standing back in the kitchen, nervously chewing a finger.

The plainclothesman turned out to be that friends of Som-Marie's they had seen at the Oriental. Nice looking Thai, slim, about thirty, Stony figured, wearing an inexpensive light tan suit. He wasn't smiling.

"Mister McGraw, I must ask you to come down to my office for questioning in regard to your wife's murder." He spoke excellent English.

"Am I under arrest?"

"Yes sir, you are. And now we must check you for weapons and put these on you." He gestured to one of the officers who came forward with a pair of handcuffs. The

128

officers appeared to be nervous to Stony, who put up his hands in a halting gesture.

"I'll go with you, but not in handcuffs."

"It is standard procedure, Mister McGraw, and you are hardly in a position to refuse," the plainclothes said, nodding towards the uniforms, who were all slightly built men.

Stony tried to bluff, "There are only seven of you," he said taking a defensive stance, hands on his hips.

There was a short staring contest.

"Alright, Mister McGraw, in the interest of diplomatic courtesy we will forego procedures. However, you will ride in the backseat of a patrol car with a policeman on either side of you, with weapons drawn. If you make any attempt to escape, they will shoot you."

"Fair enough." Stony gave a reassuring glance to the maid, "Take care of things around here, I'll be back." She didn't answer, just stood there in the kitchen looking frightened. Her husband had probably slipped away at first sight of the police.

Stony climbed into the backseat of one of the patrol cars, an officer sat on each side of him. It was a tight fit. Before entering they each pulled out military looking 45's. He noticed that neither of them cocked their weapon, which appeared rather large in their small hands. They looked very uncomfortable so he smiled at each and said, "Sawat dii," the Thai version of hello. He didn't bring his hands up in the accompanying prayer like gesture – no unnecessary movements – they looked nervous enough. He tried to put them at ease by appearing to be very casual on the long hot ride downtown.

Once at the sprawling police department building, Stony was escorted to the second floor rear corner office of his arresting officer. It was a large room, like any big city squad room, several desks and a holding cell in one corner. Overhead fans and open windows were the only ventilation. It was going to be a long, hot day. Once inside, all but two of the uniforms were dismissed. Stony was directed to a small table with a couple of chairs. He sat in one.

"Isn't your name Lang?" Stony asked the plainclothesman.

"Lang Pibul, Mister McGraw, *Captain* Lang Pibul. This is an official inquiry; I would prefer that you call me Captain Pibul."

"Fine. But you're barking up the wrong tree, Captain Pibul. Not only did I have nothing to do with my wife's death, but I have been looking for the killers myself for a year."

"We have information to the contrary, Mister McGraw." He opened a folder and began to spread its papers on the table. Stony glanced at them but they were all in Thai. And the questioning began. It was polite but thorough. Stony went along with it, feeling he really didn't have much of a choice. He cooperated and filled in some of the police department's missing information, when he felt it didn't hurt his own efforts. There were, now and then, bits of information he gleaned for his own use from the way the questions were formed. He had to omit any classified information of course, but the questioning really didn't get into those areas much anyway. To the police this was a murder to be solved and they didn't seem to regard any espionage angle to be important. Polite but relentless. Over and over he repeated countless small details of their lives since arriving in Bangkok eighteen months ago.

At lunch, his questioner took a break and left. Shortly an older woman arrived carrying a tray. She lifted a towel to reveal a bowl of fried rice, some fish and a small pot of green tea. She set it down, put her hands together as in prayer and bowed slightly in the Thai greeting gesture called a wai. Stony retuned the gesture. What he really wanted was something cold to drink.

"You understand Green Spot?"

"Green Spot," she nodded affirmatively. Stony held up two fingers and handed her a 10 baht note. She wai'd again and left. Stony ate the fried rice, took a couple sips of the tea and offered the fish to one of the uniforms, who gratefully took it. The lady returned in a few minutes with the two soft drinks and Stony let her keep the tip of about forty cents. The orange drinks were cool but really too sweet to satisfy a thirst. He didn't think he could get away with ordering a beer.

Captain Pibul returned and the questioning resumed. Stony had seen it in the movies where they try to break a suspect's story by repeatedly asking for the same information. He thought it was only in the movies. Not so. Always polite, but always unrelenting.

"How about a phone call, Captain. I should let my office know where I am."

"This is not America, Mister McGraw. Our laws are a combination of French and British laws and some of our own that we have developed over time. You are not guaranteed any telephone calls. However, in due time, I will permit you to call your embassy. Remember, this is not just a questioning session, Mister McGraw, you are under arrest for the murder of your wife."

"Why now? I've been here for a year since then and could have left at any time. If you have been checking on me you would know I have been pursuing an investigation of my own. Why arrest me now?"

"This has been a very difficult investigation so far. Your embassy has been of no help whatsoever, in fact it has seemed at times that they have been hindering it. We have just recently developed new information with which I believe we can successfully close this case."

"Like what?" Stony hoped for the answer.

"That I cannot reveal to you at this time."

"Just what I thought, an informant."

Captain Pibul shot a quick involuntary glance at Stony.

"Bingo!"

"Now let's begin at the beginning," and the mind-numbing process began again.

Late in the afternoon, Pibul carefully rearranged all the papers back into the folder, "Let's talk about that terrible argument you and your wife had just before she was killed."

"Terrible argument? We didn't have a terrible argument."

"According to our information, you did."

"That's not the way it was. Something had been bothering her for two days, really bothering her, and she wouldn't talk about it. It wasn't like her not to talk about something to me. We had always talked. I knew it had to be something pretty bad, so I pushed it a little that day. I insisted she tell me what was bothering her. We had some words about it. Not really much of an argument. She refused to talk about it and left."

Stony felt himself getting upset as he relived the scene. He had regretted those last unpleasant words ever since. The last conversation they had, after all those years of a great marriage, was in anger.

"Where was she going?"

"To the beauty shop. The one below the Derby Club. We were going out that night and it was one of the few personal pleasures she got over here. Sometimes I would go with her and have a couple beers upstairs at the Derby. If only…"

"If only what?"

"Nothing." He felt foolish for even saying it. If he had accompanied her they would both be dead.

"And you didn't want her to go."

"What? Come off it, Captain. Don't start fishing. You've got the picture, let it go."

"Alright, Mister McGraw, answer this question. How much insurance did you carry on your wife?"

"You don't really think…"

"People have been murdered for insurance. How much?"

"Oh for…, a hundred thousand."

"That is a large amount of money. It was a new policy, was it not?"

"Not so new. We bought it before we left the U.S. And in our situation it wasn't as much money as it might seem."

"This could support premeditation. Do you realize that?"

"You know, I'm getting tired of all this. I want a phone call or a lawyer, and I want one or the other damn quick!"

"Or what, Mister McGraw? I remind you this is not America. I have tried to treat you like a gentleman. I do not hate you, this is my job. If we could develop another suspect or if we could develop some mitigating circumstances, I would be happy to pursue that. We believe we have all the evidence necessary to convict you, Mister McGraw, I am merely attempting to fill in the missing information."

"Well, I may be naïve, but I always felt that the truth is the only way to any solution."

In a more conciliatory tone, "Could you tell me why you thought you needed that much insurance on your wife?"

"Sure. I can tell you. When I took this job, we sat down and made some financial decisions. We looked forward to coming to Bangkok, but we were realistic enough to realize that accidents happen."

"Accidents?"

Stony ignored the inflection. "So we took out a new life insurance policy to supplement the small policy we already had. I felt that as the breadwinner, I should have a larger amount, so I have $250,000 on me so that if I died the bank and the ranch would be paid off with a little to spare. My wife insisted on her hundred thousand to insure the future of the kids. If you want to know, there are also small policies on my children. Does that satisfy you, Captain?"

Pibul looked pensive for a moment. He began shaking his head and in a somewhat sympathetic tone, he asked, "Did you ever figure out what might have been bothering her?"

"No. Afterwards it didn't seem to be very important anymore. It was bad enough that we parted angry."

"It might have been, Mister McGraw. It might still be."

Stony looked intently as Captain Pibul. He wasn't the enemy. He really was just doing his job, and he was good at it. Now he had just given Stony something to ponder.

At six o'clock, Captain Pibul looked at his watch.

"I must go now, but we will take this up again in the morning. You will remain here in the office; we have a temporary detention facility over there," Pibul nodded towards the holding cell. "As a courtesy to you I will not have you kept in the general jail population. You have been very reasonable, Mister McGraw. Honestly, I expected some trouble. So, if you do not wish to eat the food provided, I will send an officer to procure a meal that you would prefer, as long as you pay for it, of course."

"That's genuinely civil of you, Captain. I do appreciate it. Let me ask you to translate my order. Since I don't think your man will understand. How about sending him over to Mario's near the Erawan Hotel for a meatball sandwich and a couple of beers."

Pibul smiled. Mister McGraw, you can't be serious. I can't allow... Oh I suppose it could do no harm, but only one beer."

"You are a true gentleman, Captain Pibul; I could really get to liking you, in other circumstances, of course."

"Of course. Now, if you please," Pibul gestured towards the cell. Stony complied. Pibul called in an officer and directed him as requested. As the officer glanced toward Stony, he quickly held up two fingers and gestured with his hand that he included the officer in the beer. The officer grinned, he got the message.

As he waited for his supper, Stony leaned back on the small bunk and began to plot his escape. It was a real bummer having only an 'official' passport. With a diplomatic one he wouldn't be in this mess. Unable to contact anyone, he'd have to do this himself. With all the extra work Allan had laid on him, they might not be overly worried about him yet at the office. Unless the maid had contacted someone, but she might not know how. It was still too early yet, too much activity in the building. Only one officer guarding him. Later, he thought, late in the night. He still had his boot gun. Yea, late in the night.

The officer returned with supper. Grinning broadly he produced three beers from his sack along with the meatball sandwich. Stony took only one beer, letting the officers have the other two. He was tired enough and didn't want to take any chance of falling asleep. He also let the cop keep the two dollars worth of change from the hundred baht note he had given Pibul. Thai cops are paid poverty wages, even for Thailand, so they are expected to supplement their wages in their own imaginative ways. Some do quite well by accommodating wealthy business clients. Stony had once been required to attend a cocktail party at an obviously wealthy police official's estate. It was very elegant, plenty of servants, manicured grounds, excellent food and liquor. Later he learned the 'police official' was only a corporal. It's no wonder the man on the street sees the whole system as corrupt.

After awhile one cop left. The other turned on a small black and white TV set on a corner desk and was soon engrossed in it. Stony decided to bide his time until after the next shift change. He didn't know the length of the shifts and didn't want to risk an interruption of his plans. He lay on the bunk, face to the wall, fighting sleep. Finally, at midnight his guard was relieved and the new guy, after a few moments was also engrossed in the little television. Stony decided to let him settle in, get comfortable and relaxed.

It was close to one o'clock when Stony decided it was time. He slowly eased the boot pistol out and tucked it in his belt. He needed something to bring the guard over, but not alarm him enough to summon help. They hadn't taken his supper trash; maybe if he dropped the beer bottle and broke it …maybe he could pick up the glass pieces and get the officer to take it for him. When he got close enough…

Suddenly, the door flew open. It was JJ?

Yes! It was JJ. In an instant he had his gun at the cop's head and his finger to his lips. He disarmed him and forcefully escorted him to the cell. Not a word was spoken. The cop nervously opened the cell without further urging. JJ pulled a gag and some rope from his pocket. They bound and gagged the unfortunate officer and locked him in the cell.

"Had to wait until the cleaning crews turned out enough lights. This is the only lit up room on this floor. We'll have to go out a window, there's a pipe I think we can use by that second window over there to the right." He leaned out and found the pipe.

"Yea, there it is. Let's get out of here." They scrambled down the pipe and ran to JJ's waiting car, just down the alley.

"We'll go straight to the embassy and I'll drop you off. Don't know how much time we've got before they discover you're gone. Here, dump these in the classified trash so they'll burn." He handed Stony a snap-brim cap and paste-on mustache. "Simple, but effective. I don't think that poor cop could pick me out again."

"JJ, you're the cavalry to the rescue. I was about to implement my own plan but I don't know if it would have worked." He pulled the pistol out of his belt and held it up.

"I'll be damned. Always thinking, Stony, that's what I like about you."

"So how'd you know?" They were on Ploenchit Road now, close to the embassy, driving as fast as they dared.

"Your maid. Allan called your house and got no answer. But with your reputation for straight arrow, he didn't pursue it. I decided to check you out; things are too strange right now. Talked to your maid, what I could. She said police took you away. At first I thought I wasn't understanding her right. She was plenty scared. I went to the central Police Department and asked to see you. Of course they wouldn't cooperate. So I went higher up, to the Interior Ministry and sort of played the role as an embassy official irate that one of our staff was being held incognito. They checked around and gave me the name of a Captain Pibul and his office room number. I didn't want to put anyone on guard, but I could tell it was on the second floor, so I just waited until I could narrow it down from the outside. Just kept driving around and checking every ten minutes or so. The rest, my friend…"

They entered the embassy grounds without incident. The Thai policeman on guard hardly looked up.

"They'll figure this out soon enough, JJ, but they can't do anything about it now that I'm here. I do need a favor though. Do you think you could go by my house and get me a change of clothes? Oh, and my 38 is wedged up under the driver's seat of my car. Just honk at the gate and the maid will let you in. Tell her I'm alright and give her this money, don't know when I'll see her again. She knows you so there shouldn't be any problem."

"Can do, Kemo Sabe. I'll fill a suitcase with what I can find."

"Better hurry, they'll check the house first."

He signed in with the Marine Security Guard and headed up the stairs towards the office. JJ was back within an hour.

"Your maid thought it was you. I hated to disappoint her, but I think she realizes you are going to be alright now. You got a good girl there."

"I owe you one for all this, JJ. Right now I'm going down to the DCM's office and make use of his shower. Then I'm

138

going to catch a few winks on the office cot. You think you'll be ok sleeping at home?"

"Nobody saw me but that one cop and I don't think he would recognize me. They might want to question me, but what would I know?"

Since their office only had a toilet and a sink, Stony made use of the Deputy Chief of Mission's (sort of a deputy ambassador) full bath down on the second floor. Since it was now after 3 AM, he went ahead and shaved, to save a little time later. Although exhausted, he didn't sleep well on the office cot, and just before seven, he got up, and put everything away.

He realized he was severely hampered now. His effectiveness was going to be near zero. He had lost. He was trapped within his own embassy. Sitting in a chair, his head in his hands, he made a decision. Slowly, reluctantly, he composed a short message to his agency monitor, Richard Ireland. Messages were the COS's job, but he just didn't want to face Allan's gloating right now. He finished it and dropped it off at the embassy's communications center for priority posting to Washington. He picked up a couple of rolls at the cafeteria and returned to the office to make some coffee.

He was cleaning his weapon when Allan came in.

"Use it?"

"No. Just keeping it happy."

It was nothing fancy like a lot of other agents carried. The new James Bond books had everybody buying Walther PPK's, but after trying one, he found that for a careful shot, the trigger pull was a little too hard and interfered with accuracy. No, his was just a snubbed-nose Smith & Wesson 38 caliber pistol. Not too heavy, small enough to be easily concealed inside pleated slacks or an ankle holster, with enough firepower to get the job done. Heavier weapons were difficult to conceal here in the tropics where nobody wore jackets of any kind. Except, of course, the Secret Service when they were in town. Most agents preferred the automatics. Stony, always feeling he was an armchair exile from the 1880's, opted for a revolver. Keep it simple, keep it clean, repairs were easy, and it won't jam on you like the automatics sometimes do.

"You're in early," said Allan, "after the way you've been running the past few days, I didn't expect to see you this morning."

"Why not?" Stony stared intently at Allan.

"Well, I mean…, by the way, where were you all day yesterday? If it had been anyone else, I'd have sent out the dogs."

"Busy, Allan. Just busy," he poured himself some coffee. He needed answers and he wasn't acknowledging anything until he had to.

The phone rang. Allan stepped out to answer it. The phone was in a sound proof booth in the entrance room, where cover music was always played, for security reasons.

"The DCM wants to see me immediately. Said it concerned one of my men."

"That'd be me, Allan; I probably left my razor down there."

Allan glanced at him quizzically, but said nothing. It wasn't much of a gamble, but Stony wanted to be there for this conversation.

The Deputy Chief of Mission was a career diplomat whose main job was to see that the political appointee Ambassador didn't screw up. The State Department saw to it that there was always a competent diplomat behind each political appointee. Most expected to step up into ambassadorship in one of the less glamorous countries eventually. A very experienced man, Allison S. Smithe usually handled the tough calls. Tweedle Dee, the secretaries called him because of his rotund build topped by a completely bald head. They called the General Services Officer, Tweedle Dum because they resembled each other, but the GSO was less well liked.

The DCM was somewhat taken aback as Stony stepped into his office with Allan.

"Well, Mister McGraw, I am quite surprised to see you. There must be some mistake. I was informed by the Thai Interior Ministry that you were under arrest."

"Imagine that. All I can say is here I stand, sir. If you would like, I would be glad to check it out for you. Discreetly."

"Well, I have…, hmmm; certainly, you could manage to look into the matter more discreetly than an official inquiry by my staff. In that case, I will await your finding."

As they entered the hallway, Allan turned to Stony, "Is there something you should be telling me, I am the boss, you know."

"Well, The Boss, I may have something for you soon." Still buying time. How long would it last? As he walked back into the office, he mused about what exactly was going on. He had expected the escaped prisoner alarm to have been sounded by the local police and the posse set loose by now. Except for a little CYA by the Interior Ministry, probably set in motion by JJ's inquiries yesterday, nothing seemed to be happening. He hadn't seen any paperwork about an arrest, not signed any paperwork, nor been photographed, or finger-printed while in custody. It could be that he hadn't really been under formal arrest. Maybe Captain Pibul was acting mostly on his own. JJ's questions may have initiated some internal inquiries among the Thai police authorities. It was Stony's guess that until they picked up the informant, that they couldn't proceed on an official basis yet. Maybe the informant couldn't be found now, if there ever was one.

They were probably looking for him alright, but were keeping it low-level to avoid being embarrassed. They would certainly check his place, question the police guards at the embassy and since Pibul knew about Som-Marie, she would be under surveillance. He decided to stay close to the office, even within the embassy. No locals were allowed on the third floor, where most classified activities occurred, so he could move freely there. He would confine his showers to late night after the cleaning crew locals went home. He hadn't been seen yet, except by two cafeteria workers, who didn't know who he was and he hadn't encountered any locals on the trip to the DCM's office. He would lay low until he came up with a new plan. Never give up, never give up.

Meanwhile, Allan had stopped off at the embassy communications center for his morning check for messages. When he entered the office Stony watched as he immediately decoded a message, stared at it for a long moment, and shredded it. He lit a cigarette and left saying he had something urgent to attend to. As he opened the door to leave, "Whoa, Allan. Just in case I need to know, does it have anything to do with that message?"

"Yes, as a matter of fact, it did. But it was personal for the Ambassador. I'll be out for awhile."

Not so unusual, thought Stony, his office was often used as a backchannel for classified or personal information for the Ambassador. It was part of their job. In fact, the Ambassador was the only other embassy official allowed into their office, even though he was only given information on the usual 'need to know' basis.

CHAPTER 8

The door flew open and in came Pete, John and JJ, laughing and joking.

"You boys running a little late this morning aren't you?" teased Stony.

"Aw, hell, we were already late when we saw Allan leaving so we went back for another cup of coffee. But we brought you a nice sweet roll. Here, catch," said Pete as he threw a napkin covered roll to Stony.

"Talk to Allan yet?" asked JJ.

"No," answered Stony, while pouring another cup of coffee. He sat down, took a bite of his roll, "but I figure we might as well let these two characters know, before they find out accidentally and spill the beans prematurely."

He related the previous day's events to the three of them, including the visit to the DCM's office this morning, and requested the favor that they not tell Allan.

"As soon as he finds out he'll have my plane ticket home in a heartbeat. I need whatever time I can get to develop a plan."

"How much do you really think you can do, Stony," asked John, "hiding out here in the embassy and on the lam from the law?"

"That's just it, John, I don't know if I am really on the lam from the law, officially, that is. It might just be Pibul and his men out looking for me. No APB. If I could figure out how to elude them, I might be able to function."

"Sounds like a 'no chancer' to me, Stony," added Pete. "You ain't much of a chair-sitter and it won't take long for Allan to figure out you've taken up a home here."

"Pete's right Stony. We need to get you out of here. Anybody got any ideas?" asked JJ.

"Well," offered John, "Pete and I have the little 'kill 'em' mission to Nam tonight maybe you could ride along and just hang out in Nam for a few days."

"By damn, John, that's a pretty pregnant idea you've got there," chimed Pete, "let's brainstorm that baby to full term."

"Funny thing," said Stony, "I'm getting so claustrophobic in these windowless rooms that I was thinking of sleeping up under that heliport tonight. You guys just might have something."

The phone rang. JJ got it and returned to the room. "It's for you Stony, a woman."

Four puzzled faces, accompanied by two smirks. Stony went out, closed the door to the sound-proof booth, "Hello. Who is this?"

"Oh, Stony. It is Som-Marie. I am so happy to hear your voice. I need to talk to you. I asked the Marine if he could call your office, he is very kind. I need very much to see you."

He wanted to see her, too. But. Oh hell, there are times to break the rules, and this was one of them.

"Som-Marie, I'm going to have you brought upstairs. Let me speak to the Marine Guard."

"Stony, Steve here. This lady seems a little upset."

"I don't doubt it Steve. Could you get her an escort to the third floor? Quietly. I'll take the heat."

"Can do. Just be there to accept her." Stony returned to the group.

"You guys work on that plan, please. I'll be in the conference room if you need me."

The conference room on the third floor was a lockable secure room used when it was necessary to discuss privileged information with uncleared personnel. Since no foreign nationals were allowed on the third floor, he would be breaking the rules, but not breaching security. There was a naked red light bulb above the door that was lit when the room was in use, to let it be known that uncleared personnel were on the floor. It was just a precaution, since all classified activities were supposed to take place behind locked doors. He checked the room and flipped on the light.

Corporal Steve had escorted Som-Marie himself. "Needed a little exercise break."

Som-Marie leapt forward and embraced Stony in a lock grip. As Steve turned to leave the room, he raised his eyebrows in admiration; Stony could only lamely grin in return.

He took her into the room where they just held each other for awhile. She was shaking; he felt her tears on his shirt. When she found a tissue, he took it from her hand and gently dabbed her tears. He bent down slightly and gently kissed her below the corner of each eye.

"Easy now," he whispered, "it's going to be alright." He slowly stroked her hair. Eventually she could talk. Still upset, choking back her anguish,

"Oh Stony, I have been so worried. Last night I tried to call you, but after many rings your maid answered. She said the police had arrested you and taken you away. She was very distressed and I could not help her. I couldn't sleep all night. This morning I called my friend Lang, you remember him? Well he was not any help. Only after I begged him to find you, he would only say that he would look into it. I didn't know what to do. I desperately needed to know if you were alright. I thought maybe if I could speak to someone in your office, they might help. So on the pretense of applying for a visa, I came to the consulate. When I received my paperwork, I walked through the doors into the embassy. I saw the phone on the Marine Guard's desk, so I asked if he could call you. That way I hoped to speak to someone in your office. He was very kind. Then when I heard your voice, I almost lost my composure." She blurted it all out, crying some, sniffling. He pulled her close and held her. With the back of his hand he was wiping away some tears of his own. She held onto him tightly and seemed so vulnerable right now that he wished he would never have to let her go.

He would have to tell her eventually, so he took hold of her shoulders and looked into her dark, wet eyes.

"I have something to tell you." He sat down in a plush leather chair and pulled her onto his lap. He told her about the arrest and the escape.

"I can't leave the embassy grounds now because I can't risk re-arrest here in Bangkok. We've sort of decided that I should go away for a few days and see what develops."

"Go away? Where?"

"I'm not sure. Maybe Vietnam."

"Maybe Ko Samet!"

"Maybe where?"

"Ko Samet. It is an island south of Rayong, further south than Pattaya. My uncle owns a bungalow there and I go once or twice a year to get away. That's what we could do, get away. No one would need to know where you are. There are no police. But you would need a way to get out of here."

"That's not a problem, and you just may have something. Wait here just a minute." He kissed her and went to his office.

"Boys, grab your coffee cups. I want you to meet somebody – who means a lot to me – and we just might have a plan developing."

He introduced them to her, told her to remember their names and faces, that they were the only ones to be trusted. They began to work out a little plan.

First, Pete would send a message to the office in the Saigon embassy. They would in turn, send a commercial cable to Captain Lang Pibul in which he would be informed that Stony was now in Saigon. That could cause him to drop the search. Maybe. Tonight, at seven, Pete and John would board the chopper atop the embassy accompanied by Stony and Som-Marie, who would exit at Sattahip and taxi to Rayong. JJ would handle Allan, by feigning ignorance if nothing else. JJ would cash a check for Stony at the embassy cashier. Since Stony already had his suitcase packed, courtesy of JJ, he was set.

"Now pretty lady, you need to take your visa paperwork home, fill it out and return it by 4:30 this afternoon. That will give you an excuse to return. Meanwhile, maybe you could put on one of those muumuus and secrete under its billowing volume some clothes for the trip."

"What a great idea! Except that I wouldn't own one of those things," she smiled, "besides, it is an isolated beach. What would I need?"

"Please, you are embarrassing my friends. Pete, would you please escort my lady back downstairs?"

Back in the office, they got out the maps. Ko Samet was a small, elongated, forested island, pie shaped, with the narrow tip on the southern end, less than three miles wide and narrowing quickly to only about a quarter mile wide for the rest of its five mile length; few people with only one sizable village, Na Dan, towards the northern end. They would be staying in a bungalow near the beach of Ao Wai, about two-thirds down towards the very narrow southern end. Few facilities, but there was a phone line to the mainland from Na Dan. Stony would check in each day. How many days – they would play it by ear.

"By the way, you sly fox, when did you luck into a dish like that?"

"She's quite something isn't she? Just the other night, but things kinda developed speedy-like."

"That's got to be one of the finest looking ladies I've seen in Thailand. And smart too. About time things got better for you 'ol buddy."

"Better? Remember, I'm on the lam from the law, JJ."

"Oh, that's right. You poor fellow. You're going to spend a couple days on a tropical island with a beauty queen who's crazy about you. Yep, you've got it real tough, Stony." Stony did have to smile at that comment.

"By the way, I sent that wire to Richard Ireland back at headquarters. He should be answering anytime. Let me know what he says, will you?"

"Sure. By the way, supper's on me tonight. I'll pick up a few orders of Kobe beef from the Imperial and we can eat in the conference room while we wait. That is, if you don't mind a third thumb joining you lovebirds. Figure you'll have plenty of time alone later."

"That'd be great, JJ. And I want you to know that while I'm lying around on that beach, I'll be thinking of you."

"Aw, shaddap."

"Wonder what Allan's been up to all day? Since he never did come back to the office," said JJ as he wiped his mouth and picked up his beer. Shortly after five he had brought three dinners of Kobe beef from the Imperial Hotel's restaurant, the Emerald Grill, including a bottle of French burgundy and a Singha beer for himself.

"Never learnt to like wine myself. Hope you drink wine ma'am. Figured a sophisticated lady like you probably would though."

"Thank you JJ. Yes, I do enjoy wine occasionally," Som-Marie answered.

They sat around one corner of the large conference table. Since the conference room was seldom used, the central air-conditioning overly cooled it. It was a large room, probably fifteen feet square, paneled in polished Teakwood, which was overlaid with large framed squares of deep green Thai silk.

Stony filled Som-Marie's and his glasses. He had just retrieved one of his shirts from his suitcase and draped it around her shoulders. She gratefully accepted.

He answered JJ, "Who knows, maybe he ran into his friend. You know how lovers can lose track of time."

"Oh. Your boss has a girlfriend?"

"Not exactly," they both chimed. When they both smirked, she obviously decided not to pursue the subject.

Pete and John arrived at 6:45, not in their usual jovial moods. They were each wearing dark pullover shirts and jeans.

"You guys look a little down. Sorry to see 'ol Stony go?" teased JJ.

"Naw, that wouldn't bother us. But this is serious business tonight," answered Pete.

"JJ, there just ain't nothin' amusin' about killin," offered John.

"Well before you boys say anymore, let's head up to the roof," said Stony. He picked up his suitcase, which was really nothing more than a small duffel bag with strap handles. Som-Marie carried only an oversized purse. They trooped upstairs and out into the hot, humid night air.

"Sure makes you appreciate air-conditioning doesn't it? By the way, Som-Marie, ever ridden in a helicopter before?" asked JJ as the chopper settled onto the helipad above them. She just shook her head negatively, the noise and downdraft drowning out any chance of conversation. JJ gave Stony a long serious look then flashed the thumbs up sign as they climbed the stairs.

Stony helped Som-Marie get seated, and then strapped her in. She looked worriedly at each side and then at Stony, obviously unnerved that both sides of the chopper were open. She kept a lock-grip on Stony's hand the whole trip.

The chopper jockey was older than the first one and they took off with a more reasonable lift.

At Sattahip, Pete and John jogged over to the waiting Air Force jet while Stony and Som-Marie caught a ride with a member of the ground crew to the front gate. There they flagged down a taxi for the half-hour trip to Rayong and then the fifteen mile ride to the seaside village of Ban Phe. They exited the taxi near the pier.

"We can stay in a hotel tonight here in Ban Phe and take a boat over in the morning, or I might be able to find a man I know who will take us out tonight, but it will cost more. What do you think?"

"Considering the situation, it might be better to go tonight," answered Stony.

They began walking down the street and Som-Marie asked in several stores and street side restaurants for the man named Tuan. Finally she found him, playing cards with several friends. He gave her a friendly wave and after a short conversation, agreed to take them to the island. They would leave in one hour.

"It will cost 250 Baht. Is that alright?"

"No problem. Why don't we get something to eat and then pick up some supplies." Som-Marie picked out a restaurant and also picked out the food, most of which tasted just fine.

"We will need some mosquito coils and bug repellant. Also some drinking water and food. I don't think we could find your wine here in Ban Phe, and the beer would get too warm, but we could get some local whiskey if you would like. There is no electricity in the little house, but we have kerosene lamps. There is a man named Tavi who looks after the place when we are away. If you like to swim, there is some snorkeling equipment also."

"Whoa, slow down there. Don't worry yourself about all that. I'm just looking forward to a couple of uninterrupted days with you; anything else will just be a distraction. And no, we don't have to drink."

She gave an impish smile. They picked up what they thought they needed and met the boat man, Tuan, at the pier.

The boat was small, not over fifteen feet, and shallow drafted. It was powered by a healthy four cylinder engine. Stony hoped the sea was smooth. It was. The only light was a pole-mounted lantern on the prow. The map showed Ko Samet to be about four kilometers from shore; the slow progress of the night passage made it seem a lot longer. Eventually he could make out the silhouette of the island against the night sky. The boat slowed and grounded itself on the beach. Tuan helped them unload and after a friendly conversation with Som-Marie embarked for the return trip.

"It isn't far; I'll show you the way." She picked up what she could and led the way through the unusually crunchy sand toward the tree line. Stony dutifully followed with the rest of the gear. The little house was at the very edge of the tree line and once there, Som-Marie fumbled around in her purse for a match. She found one and used the light to find a lantern and lit it. Then she lit two more. Stony looked around. The house was small, with one general purpose room, simple kitchen in the corner and one other room, a bedroom. It was concrete constructed, with a flat concrete roof. He learned later that the back half of the roof had a short wall around it and was tar coated. This was an ingenious way of catching rain water and heating it by the sun for bathing. The toilet was outside on the back wall, a 'one-holer' as they say. The place was sparsely furnished, as you would expect a vacation house to be; a table and four chairs toward one side and four rattan easy chairs around a low table near the door. Several cabinets hung on the wall near the kitchen corner. The bedroom had only a double bed and a simple table. Som-Marie opened the windows; three in this room, two in the bedroom, but it was still stuffy. She busied herself taking care of things and then opened a cabinet and took out sheets, placing them on a low table. She began to undress.

"Are you going to sleep in your clothes, sir?" She grinned teasingly. Stony obediently undressed and they strode out the door into the darkness, stark naked.

"I know a much more pleasant place to sleep." She led the way down through the soft dry sand, almost to where it solidified near the water, carrying the sheets and a lantern. She knelt down, made a couple of sand pillows, with the lantern above them and spread one of the sheets out. She shook out the other one and Stony lay down on the beachside bed. She lay down beside him, the second sheet settled over them. They lay there, holding each other; the only sound was the surf gently lapping at the shore, and the whisper of their own breathing which slowly, ever so slowly, grew heavier.

They awoke to the rising tropic sun. Stony sat up and looked around. They were near the edge of an almost still, blue-green sea. Bright, white sand stretching away in both directions to the edge of the shallow cove they inhabited. Behind them was the small concrete house, shadowed by the trees. Otherwise they were completely alone.

"Would you care to join me in an early morning swim?" He smiled down at Som-Marie, utterly beautiful in the morning light. They cavorted nakedly in the comfortably warm sea for a while. Stony couldn't help but keep a lookout for an approaching boat or beach strollers, to the amusement of Som-Marie. Afterwards, at the house, she lit the two-burner counter top stove and made coffee. There was a little water in the roof fed shower, so they cleaned up, dressed and drank the coffee accompanied by a couple of rice cakes, out under a tree, sitting in rattan chairs that Stony had carried out. A ferry-taxi cruised by, a mile or so out, heading for the village at the northern end of the island. They sat there a long time, holding hands, saying little, enjoying the total relaxation of the moment. Eventually, Som-Marie made a suggestion.

"If you would like, we could hike to Na Dan for lunch. It's a little over an hour by the inland trail, or we could walk along the beach and then take a ferry back."

"That sounds like a good idea, sweetheart. Let's take the beach and after lunch I could check in with JJ." They had purchased cheap tennis shoes in Ban Phe. Stony hid his boot pistol in a chair cushion, the only weapon he had brought along, rolled up his pant legs to mid calf, and left his shirt unbuttoned. Som-Marie tied her blouse in a knot just below her breasts and above her matching white, loose shorts.

They strolled northward along the beach, just above the water line where the sand was firmer.

"This is a beautiful little island, Som-Marie; I'm surprised it hasn't become more popular."

"On holidays there are many more people here, but most of the time it is like this. For some reason, this island doesn't get much rain, compared to the mainland, so people just seem to expect beautiful weather for their holidays here."

"Do you know the name of these trees? They seem to be pretty thick up there," he said, gesturing towards the tree

155

line. The trees were not so very tall, but were covered with long lance-like leaves. When he had crushed a leaf in his hand, he smelled a mixture of turpentine and camphor.

"I think it is called the Cajeput tree, but we call it the Samet tree. The island is named after it. It is much in demand all around Asia but only seems to grow here and further south in the Malay Islands, and I think I heard it also grows in India. In Thai, 'ko' means island, so Ko Samet means the island of the Samet tree."

She continued, "The Forestry Department and some others are trying to get the island declared a national park before it gets too popular and developers begin to operate." She was wading ankle deep in the surf.

"They'd better act fast – developers are vultures. They won't care about the island, just how much money they can grab."

They sat down for a moment, being in no particular hurry. They were in the area known as Ao Thian or Candlelight Beach. It was so peaceful, such a contrast to Stony's tumultuous life right now. He was unable to avenge his wife's murder, unable to do his job, on the run from the law, and all this even paled with the thought of what ordinary GI's were struggling with in the bloodbath only a 45 minute jet flight away.

Som-Marie must have noticed his suddenly brooding demeanor.

"Come on," she jumped to her feet, pulling at his hand, "I'll tell you an old Thai epic tale, part of which was set on this very island."

He joined her, feeling a little ashamed of himself. He had made a conscious effort to make this trip totally enjoyable and in an instant had allowed the dark mantle of despondency to settle on him like a shroud. They began walking, holding hands again and gently swinging their arms.

She began, "You probably don't know it, but the Thai people love poetry. There was a poet named Sunthorn Phu, who wrote an epic tale that is dearly loved by the people and gave a certain prominence to this little island." She was smiling up at him, almost with the earnestness of a child who is hoping you will appreciate what they are doing for you.

As they strolled along the beach, she told the elaborate tale of a young prince of long, long ago, who had been exiled to an undersea kingdom. Once there, he found the kingdom to be ruled by a lovesick female giant, who wanted the prince very badly. Fortunately, a sympathetic mermaid helped the prince escape to the island of Samet. After much travail, he was finally able to outwit the female giant with the help of a magic flute. Stony became absorbed in her story, enjoying the tale as much as listening to her tell it.

The beaches of Ko Samet are separated by rocky headlands which must be climbed on narrow trails. Stony and Som-Marie were working their way up one. They continued strolling beaches and climbing headlands until they had crossed 'Diamond Beach' with its especially crunchy sand. They stopped for a few minutes at the temple at Laem Yai before continuing to the village of Na Dan.

"Thought we'd never get here, I'm hungry enough to eat a water buffalo," he said.

"You just may get your wish," she answered. Then with an almost childish plea in her eyes, "I know you are hungry, but would you mind if I made a little visit over to the pier? There is a shrine near it honoring Sunthorn Phu, the poet who wrote the story I told you. I would like to pay my respects."

"Sure. Tell you what; I'll wait for you on the bench over there." He had noticed a pushcart selling Green Spot orange drink so he purchased two and sat down drinking them both while he waited.

She returned shortly and said, "I know a nice restaurant on a little side street. Come on."

The restaurant was small, but had a unique cooling system. It had a double roof, the top one taking the heat of the tropic sun and the open front and rear created a slight breezeway effect, resulting in a reasonably comfortable atmosphere. They sat at the corner of a small table, in rattan chairs.

"You know, whenever we eat, I rely on you entirely and I have no idea what I'm having. Don't get me wrong, you do a great job, but this time how about telling me what I'm eating, just out of curiosity."

After a brief conversation with the waitress, she answered, "Alright, I hope I ordered enough, since you are so hungry."

When the meal began to arrive, she gave him a running account.

"They have no coffee here, so I ordered plain drinking water. I also told them to go easy on the spices, but some things will still be pretty hot. OK?"

"Whatever you say, ma'am." He grinned.

"Thai meals are almost always accompanied by plain rice and since you said you could eat a buffalo, this is laap neua, or spicy beef salad, and this is kai phat phrik, chicken fried with chilies. Be careful with that." She continued pointing out the dishes. "This is phak bung fai, or morning glory vine fried in garlic, chili and bean sauce. And this last one is kaeng kai naw mai, chicken curry with bamboo shoots. Hope you like curry, I love it."

"Well, I asked for it. I appreciate that you didn't order any seafood. I think I'd have passed up a fish meal, hungry as I am," Stony said as he loaded his plate from the common bowls.

"I know," she leaned close and whispered, "they probably think we are crazy since this is an island and seafood is the cheapest thing on the menu."

The food was good and the cook had obviously held back on the spices, for which he was grateful. Still, he did drink three glasses of the barely cool water as he consumed a good two-thirds of the food on the table.

"You really were hungry, weren't you. I was thinking that maybe tomorrow we could hire a boat and do some skin-diving around the nearby uninhabited islands. It is as beautiful underwater here as it is above."

"Gee, I don't know, Som-Marie, if the boat has a skipper we would have to wear swimsuits," he teased.

She just grinned and shook her head. "Come on, Mister Nudist, I'll show you the way to the public phone office."

They made their way down a side street and around a corner to a plain, off-white, stucco, one floor building. A few minutes after she had made the arrangements with the clerk, Stony heard JJ's voice on the other end.

"How's the honeymoon, 'ol buddy?"

"The *vacation* is just fine. What's happening back there?"

"Well, it's big news but bad news. Allan's been kidnapped. Found a ransom note in his apartment. No real info in it. Just to wait for them to contact us. I'll explain it all when you get here. I've got a chopper set to pick you up at dawn. You still staying at Ao Wai?"

"Still there. Short vacation. We'll be ready." He glanced at Som-Marie and could see the look of concern on her face.

JJ continued, "I also talked to the Ambassador about your little misunderstanding with the local law. Not exactly all of it but he has agreed to let you and your local 'assistant' hole up in his guest house. I told him you would be critical to Allan's rescue. He also agreed to keep this all in-house for the time being. I figure your help would be better than the local law's, and we obviously couldn't have both. So at least you have a 'safe-haven' operating base. By the way, the old boy is supporting us all the way on this. I think he's enjoying it."

"Good job, JJ. Do me a favor, call Wirey, you know, the professor, and see if he can get me a local car to rent, on the sly, preferably one with tinted windows. And one more thing, start closing down my house. Not much there, I shipped everything but the rattan furniture and bed home when the kids left. If you would, pack up my personal things and bring them to the embassy. Give the furniture to the maid. The weights, bench, air-conditioner, and bar, do with what you want. If nothing else, there are always some new people who might want them. I know I'll be there tomorrow, but if I am to maintain the ruse that I left town, I can't do it myself anyway, and I want to get the process started as soon as possible to reinforce Captain Pibul's impression that I'm really gone. I know it's asking a lot, can you do it?"

"Can do. I'll stop by tonight and tell your maid. If I can get it across. There's a new guy in the Army Attaché Office, maybe he'll want the stuff. Of course, any liquids in the bar will be confiscated, you know."

"Of course. Can you give the maid and her husband a thousand Baht apiece? That's a little more than three months

160

wages, and tell them the rent is paid for another month. Guess you might as well give the landlord the 30 days notice. Oh, and ask Wirey if he could sell my car, will you?"

"Gee, Stony, want me to give your maid a little kiss on the cheek too? After all that talking and hand signaling, I'm gonna need extra food and drink tonight – and it's gonna be on you."

"Have a blast. See you for breakfast."

He hung up the phone and turned to Som-Marie, "Summer's over. Got new problems. On the plus side, how would you like to spend some time in the American Ambassador's guest house, servants and all?"

"If it is with you, I don't care where we go."

Instead of a boat taxi, they hired one of the island's few samlor-taxi's which bounced them down the inland road to within a half mile of the bungalow. Hand in hand they followed the trail southward.

"We still have one other problem that I haven't worked out."

"Which is?"

"Which is you."

"I am a problem?" She took her hand from his, turned and faced him frowning. He reached for her hand, pulled it up and kissed it.

"Part of a problem. You're friend Captain Pibul is the real problem, but you may be his new target. Come to think of it, all this started after he saw us together. Maybe he likes you more than you think and this is all just jealousy in action. And another thing, you disappeared from Bangkok at the same time as I did, don't you think he might just suspect something. Oh, and what about your job?"

"Stony, please. You are getting too worried about things."

"I can't help it, Som-Marie," he had stopped walking, raising his hands slightly in a gesture of frustration, "I can walk away from all this, if worse comes to worse, but you, you may have to pay the consequences for sticking by me." It was a harsh truth, but it needed to be said. He didn't mean to be cruel, but once he had said it, he thought it might possibly shock her into thinking of her own self-interest. He realized now that he was in love with her and the thought of yet another person paying for his own actions was almost beyond endurance. Wild thoughts flashed through his mind, such as if he did something insulting, she might get angry enough to leave and thus save herself a lot of suffering. He knew the parting would have to come soon, even if only temporary, why not hurry things up and in the end he would be doing her a favor. The thought of parting caused an involuntary grimace of pain to cross his face.

She was standing right in front of him, staring up at him, tears in her eyes. "Stony. Please. I love you." Her own words seemed to surprise her. He was startled into the present.

"What did you say?"

She looked at him through teary eyes, "I... I said I love you. I don't know where it came from. You were in such pain; I couldn't stand to see you like that. It just came out." She took his hands, "But now that I've said it, I want you to know, I mean it."

He pulled her close and held her. After a moment or so he spoke, "I have an admission of my own. I've known almost from the beginning that I've been hopelessly in love with you too." They just held each other for a while.

Later, at the bungalow, while Som-Marie was busy getting the place ready for their departure in the morning, Stony was sitting outside, deep in thought. She walked over and sat on his lap. She liked to do that, it seemed.

"Let me put your mind at ease about something Mister Stony," she liked to call him that too, "first, you should give me a little credit. I have a good mind of my own, you know. When I returned home from the embassy the other day, I called the university and took some personal time, which I had coming. I told a small lie. I said I had a death in the family. Then I called Lang Pibul again and apologized for my demeanor in the first call and told him about the death in the family and that if he heard anything about you to telephone my aunt in Hua Hin because I would be staying there for a few days." She glanced up at Stony, appearing pleased with her little deception.

"Yes, but…"

"No, but. By the way, Lang Pibul is married to another college friend of mine. Happily, I believe. Now, let me finish. Then I telephoned my aunt and told her about that part of the plan and, if Lang called, which I doubted, unless he was checking on me, for her to tell him I was out at the time. I will call her tomorrow to see."

"You are a clever little fugitive, aren't you?" He smiled and kissed her.

It was late in the afternoon now, still hot, so they skinny-dipped again until dark and went to bed early, making good use of the little bedroom this time.

They were drinking coffee outside by the light of a kerosene lantern as the throbbing hum of the chopper grew closer. Stony had retrieved his pistol and put it in his bag.

They had closed down the bungalow and were ready to go. Stony put the chairs back inside and they walked down to the beach where the chopper hovered just above the sand, strewing bits of mica in the air and flattening the nearby water. A crewman helped Som-Marie in and then offered a hand to Stony. Som-Marie was no more comfortable this time than last, but the flight was short and as always, interesting to Stony.

CHAPTER 9

They were met at the foot of the helipad by JJ. He escorted them inside to the conference room, flipped on the lights, including the red hall light.

"Hellzapoppin', Stony! Still no word from the kidnappers, probably letting us sweat it for awhile. The 'professor' says 'can do' on the car. Should have it here sometime today. He didn't quote a price. Stopped by your house last night. Your maid ain't too happy about you're leaving, but I think the new guy down in the Army Attaché office will take everything you didn't give to the maid, and there's a good chance he'll take the house and maid with it. If everybody agrees. Should know that sometime today also."

"That'd be a nice package. Tell him the gardener's part of it. By the time their household goods arrive, it should all fall together. Thanks for doing that JJ, I owe you."

"Don't worry, I'll collect. By the way, you owe me twenty bucks for dinner the other night. Remember?"

"I remember. Here you go. Now how about getting Som-Marie and me settled in at the ambassador's place so I can get to work on things."

The ambassador's residence was a lushly landscaped, palatial compound not far up the street from the embassy.

The guest house was a two story affair, off to one side of the main house, with an apartment on each floor. The servants were well-trained and discreet. No one was in the upstairs apartment at the moment so they were the only guests. The large living-dining room had a well stocked bar in an alcove, no kitchen, all meals were served, including refreshments, two bedrooms, two baths. All air-conditioned.

"Now that you are ensconced in luxury, my dear, what are you going to do with yourself?" He was pouring three cups of coffee at the dining table.

"Well, for one thing, I noticed there are several classics among the books in that bookcase in the living room. But then, I don't know. This will be boring, just sitting here waiting for you to come back. I do wish I had some way of contributing." She accepted one of the cups from him.

"You could telephone your aunt to see if our Captain Pibul tried to contact her. And I'll tell you this, if we have to go anywhere outside of Bangkok to catch these kidnappers, I'll take you with us. We could sure use your help in translating and getting around. If you would care to, that is."

"Of course I would go. I don't want you getting too far away from me, you know." She sipped the hot coffee.

He leaned over and kissed her, "I'll be back as soon as possible." He left for the embassy with JJ.

In the office, the four of them, Stony, JJ, Pete and John, began a strategy session.

"Bangkok's a huge city, guys, they could have him anywhere. Hell, we don't even know if they are holding him *in* Bangkok," offered John.

JJ started chuckling as he filled his coffee mug, "As far as I'm concerned, it's good riddance. I say if they demand a reward, we offer to double it if they'll keep him."

Stony smiled at his friend, "He may be a piece of crap, JJ, but he's *our* piece of crap. Has anyone considered that it just might be better for Allan if he was the intended target?"

"What do you mean by that, Stony?" asked Pete.

"What I mean is, with the way things have been going for me, if they were after me and got the wrong guy, Allan could already be dead. Hate to say it, but we've got to consider it."

"That's another thing. Why? I mean if it was Allan they wanted, then why?" asked John, pacing.

"Good point John," answered JJ, "Why Allan? If it is money, then why haven't they contacted us? On the other hand, if it was one of our targets, they may be interrogating him. They might figure that him being the boss, he'd have the info they wanted." Now JJ too, was pacing, stabbing the air with his index finger to emphasize his points. Frustration weighed heavy in the room, and just venting that frustration was getting them nowhere. Stony figured they needed to take some kind of action.

"Dammit! We can't just sit here on our thumbs. Let's start turning over rocks until we find these slime balls. Pete, John, you've got contacts down in Chinatown and Thonburi, across the river. How about getting the word out on the street. JJ, why don't you check out the bar circuit and your own contacts, and I'll get hold of my Chinese Mafia people and get the word around there. If it's anybody in the local criminal element, they can find it. And JJ, how about getting hold of the professor. We could use his help on this too. What do you guys say?" Stony was standing now too.

"You're right, Stony. Next we'll spread the word up-country. Your Chinats can cover the west and north border regions. Pete and I can get some people working the eastern country toward Nakon Phanon," said John, whose frustration suddenly gave way to enthusiasm, "Anything is better than just sitting around, waiting."

"For now John, why don't you and Pete go over Allan's apartment with a fine toothed comb," said JJ. "I checked it out yesterday, but not very thoroughly. And one more thing," JJ grabbed a notepad and dropped it on his desk, "anybody leaves, put the time and destination and anything else important on this pad and stick it on that bulletin board. And when you're out of the office, check in often. Just in case. Don't want anybody else disappearing."

The phone rang. Everybody froze momentarily. Stony nodded to JJ. He was the senior agent, so it just seemed right to defer to him. JJ left the room to answer it and returned with a disappointed look on his face.

"Speak of the devil. It's the professor, wants to see you downstairs, Stony."

"Come with me, JJ. I'll need your help on this."

They descended the stairs; nobody in the office seemed to use the elevator. Stony stopped on the second floor and turned to JJ.

"How about bringing him up here and we'll talk to him in that sitting area over there," he said, indicating a windowed alcove with several stuffed chairs, "It'll be pretty busy downstairs and I'd just as soon be seen by as few locals as possible, for now. Captain Pibul could still be at it."

"Gotcha." JJ left and returned with the professor.

Stony stood, "Wirey, how you doing?" said Stony as the two topped the stairs, "Come on over here and let's talk."

"Sawadii, Stony. I get car you want. Dirty brown, dark window, nobody notice. Almost invisible. You want see?"

"I'll trust you on that, Wirey. How much?"

"One thousand baht, one week. Good deal, huh?" Wirey was beaming, "I park car down street by barber shop. About you car, I think I can get you good price. Don't know yet, but think so."

"Good enough." Stony paid him. "About the other matter, did you find anything out yet?"

"I tell you, he open book. But wait a minute. No my business, I know. But, you in trouble, my friend?" He handed a car key to Stony.

"Just a little, Wirey. One of your local cops thinks I had something to do with my wife's murder. Wants me in jail."

"He crazy! He crazy! Stony, why you no pay? Police no problem. You pay money, no more problem. Always work."

"Not this time, Wirey. I think he's taking it personal."

"What he name? I check around. Never know."

"Captain Lang Pibul, down at the main police headquarters. Now how about my Burmese. What can you tell me?"

"Still working. He clever guy, hard to learn about. Burmese government hide all information. You be careful him. This I know." He leaned conspiratorially closer to Stony, glancing around quickly, "He 33 year old, government agent. His wife still in Rangoon. Mother too. They got much money. He move mother to Rangoon, but have much property near Amarapura, in north country, close to Mandalay. Woman, hey! Pretty woman, huh? He lucky guy. She agent too. What they here for, I no know. Still working. They go up-country many time. I try get servant in he house, no luck. You be careful. He know martial art pretty good. See him practice Karate."

"Well nothing handles Karate like a K'gun." Stony grinned. Then in a more serious tone, "Wirey, we've got a

169

new problem. One of our men has been kidnapped. Name's Allan Huehner. We don't know exactly when, probably day before yesterday. We have a note, but it doesn't tell us anything, just that they took him. We'd appreciate it if you could dig anything up. Normal fees, of course, but be discreet. We haven't informed the police yet." He gave Wirey Allan's address and told him to poke around. He knew Wirey could get inside if he wanted.

"Okay. Much work. Burmese, police, kidnap. Much work. Cost plenty. No work free."

Stony handed him another thousand baht – about fifty dollars. "Just let us know what you find out," he said as he stood up.

Wirey stood and leaned close to Stony, "You my friend. I check police for you. No charge."

JJ escorted the dapper old man to the front door of the embassy. Stony sat down again, taking the few quiet moments to collect his thoughts. JJ returned and took the key from Stony's fingers.

"I'll go get the car. With local plates on it the guard at the gate will check me in. I'll tell him it's a loaner and I'll drive you out later. That way you can avoid contact with them."

"You're a good man, JJ. I'll wait right here. Got some thinking to do."

He leaned his tired body back in the stuffed chair and stared out the window, at nothing in particular. He heard someone bounding down the stairs. It was John, who was about to descend the next flight when he spotted Stony and wheeled around.

"Hey! Wake up cowboy. And stay right there, I'll be right back." And shortly, he was, but not alone.

"Richard!" Stony jumped to his feet at the sight of his old friend and mentor. "Why didn't you call, we could have met you at the airport."

They bear-hugged and then headed upstairs to the office where they could talk more freely.

"Old habits, Stony. Less conspicuous this way," said Richard as they reached the third floor. Richard Ireland was a very average guy in all appearances, which he worked hard at reinforcing. Five foot eleven, slightly receding brown hair, neatly cut, he was dressed in a light blue short sleeved shirt, worn outside pleated, wash and wear brown slacks. Not someone to draw a second look. He would carry a small high caliber automatic in an inside the belt holster. Where Richard stood out was inside. Stony considered him intellectually superior to anyone he had ever met and a past master at espionage.

Once inside the office, Richard declined the offered coffee as everyone found a comfortable perch.

"Wish I could have arrived sooner. I left D.C. immediately after receiving your cable, Stony, but I had a little problem to straighten out in Djakarta first. It seems that lately I am constantly putting out brush fires."

"Well, get your hose and shovel again, Richard, we've got a couple of brushfires raging here," said Stony, as he began filling him in on Allan's kidnapping and his own brush with the law.

JJ returned, gave a warm welcome to Richard, whom he had known for years, and pitched the car key to Stony.

"My non-descript temporary transportation," he said holding the key up in Richard's direction.

"Looks like crap and sounds like crap but it runs pretty good," offered JJ.

"Have you fellows developed any contingency plans?" asked Richard.

JJ replied, "As a matter of fact, we were just about to implement our plans. We're each about to launch our own investigative operations in our respective areas of intelligence and then coordinate what we find back here," said JJ, in a somewhat official sounding reply, "Pete and John will shake out their contacts in Chinatown and Thonburi, Stony, among other things, has connected recently with the local underworld and I have my own plans."

"Wait a minute! Wait just a damn minute!" It was John, sounding serious despite his infectious grin. "I have a question for Richard here."

"What's the question, John?"

"Well, as I understand it, cohabitating with a local national can jeopardize a top secret clearance, can it not?"

They were all focusing on Stony, obvious amusement on their faces. Even Stony couldn't help but grin.

"Nice to see you back to normal, John."

Richard interrupted, "To answer your question, John, yes, it could in certain circumstances. Could you be more specific?"

"All right, all right. I was going to tell him," retorted Stony. And so he did.

"I guess it's like this. Not long ago, when I was feeling pretty depressed about things, I met one of the most beautiful women I've ever seen, and she actually took a liking to me. We got pretty close, pretty fast. Then after my escape from the local law, she helped hide me out on a little island off the south coast. It could have been a great time, but Allan's kidnapping cut things short. Because of her association with me, she could be in danger from the local police, so when the ambassador offered a safe-haven residence, I brought her with me as my 'assistant.' That's pretty much it."

"Not all of it," added JJ.

"A Thai national?" asked Richard.

"Technically, yea, half Thai." Threw in JJ, "half American. Probably one of the most beautiful inter-cultural mixtures I've ever seen, and she is the finest example you'll find. Her dad once worked here in the consulate, her mother was a full professor at a local university, which, incidentally, is what this lady does. And a lady she is. When you meet her, you'll know damn quick she ain't some broad off the street."

Richard was thoughtfully rubbing his chin. "Could she claim American citizenship?"

"Don't know how that works," said Stony, "but I don't think she's interested. Said she didn't think she could ever leave Thailand for long. Now enough of that. We've got a job to do, let's get on it."

Pete and John left after a few minutes. JJ turned to Richard, "You got any ideas, we're open. In the meantime, how about I take you over to the Imperial and get you a room? Where's your luggage by the way?"

"That sounds good to me, and I left my bag with the Marine downstairs."

"When I get back Stony, I'll deliver you."

"Good enough and then how about both of you coming over to my new digs for dinner, say about 6:00?" They agreed. JJ delivered Richard and returned for Stony. Stony left his new phone number with the Marine on duty, in case they received any calls. At the guest house JJ stayed for a beer and Stony returned him to the embassy so he could pick up his own car, letting him out just down the road from the entrance gate. When he returned, he informed the servants about the dinner plans and after a shower, he and Som-Marie laid down for a little nap.

"Did you call your aunt in Hua Hin?"

"Yes I did, and Pibul didn't call. I don't know if that is a good sign or bad. I also called the university and he did call there, but left no message. Probably just checking. I sent one of the maids to my house with a key for some clothes." She nestled close to him, her head on his shoulder, and his arm around her. They lay there, under a sheet in the air-conditioned room for a couple of hours, not really sleeping, fully content to hold each other close as time evaporated, as it often does for those in love.

Just before five, the maid returned with Som-Marie's clothes. They playfully showered together and dressed for dinner. JJ and Richard arrived promptly at six o'clock.

Stony introduced Som-Marie to an obviously impressed Richard and then fixed a couple of Bourbon waters, a gin and tonic for Som-Marie, and handed an Amarit beer to JJ. The phone rang. It was the Marine Security Guard at the embassy.

"Stony, this is Corporal Conboy at the embassy. I understand I am to inform you of any calls. Well, you just got one from Joey Li. He said it was important that you contact him tonight."

"Thanks, Conboy. Much obliged for the info." He returned to the group.

"News?" asked JJ.

"Nothing unusual. Sounds like another GI might have gone AWOL with his girl. I'll have to meet my Chinese contact later tonight for more information."

JJ took a long drink from his beer, "Sounds like your long day is going to turn into a long night."

They enjoyed a delicious dinner of roast beef and afterwards, while JJ stuck to his beer, the other three indulged in another bottle of the ambassador's California burgundy. Richard learned of Som-Marie's political-science credentials and they were soon deep into a discussion of the relative merits of the parliamentary versus the congressional form of government. Stony and JJ quickly lost interest and began brainstorming angles of approach to Allan's kidnapping. Just before midnight JJ and Richard left to prowl the bar circuit 'searching for answers.' One of the servants came in and asked if there would be anything else for the night. Som-Marie asked for a pot of coffee.

They were sitting close together on the couch. Stony pulled back slightly, lifted her soft, ebony hair and began kissing the back of her neck, which he found incredibly sensuous. This soon led to some intense caressing which the servant girl accidentally interrupted as she returned with the coffee. She grinned at their obvious discomfiture, set the tray down and quietly disappeared.

"Whew! I could better use a cold shower than hot coffee right now. We were heading down a mighty fine road, pretty lady, but not one that I'd better be taking just now. Business before pleasure, they say."

"Whoever said that must have been a real stick in the mud," she answered. Stony couldn't help but laugh at how funny that old American cliché sounded coming from her. She yielded a funny grin of her own as she poured them both some coffee and handed him a cup.

"You will need to be wide awake when you get wherever you are going."

"It's just a meeting at the Barge with Joey Li for some information. Aren't you going with me?"

"I hadn't been asked," she replied coquettishly.

They arrived at the Barge a few minutes after one AM, just as the crowds from the 'regular' establishments were flooding in. The club was already in full swing with the band blaring "The Age of Aquarius" as usual, party lights spinning around the crowded room, cocktail waitresses scurrying to fill orders and the dance floor one mass gyration. Joey caught Stony's eye and they entered and nodded toward a back room. They threaded their way through the partying crowd to the back wall. Joey met them and escorted them into a small office. The clamor receded noticeably after he closed the door. Although dressed as sharply as usual, there was not smile on his face. He greeted them politely but somberly. He was already acquainted with Som-Marie through his part ownership of the Derby Club, where she was a sometime patron.

"I have news which I must give to you, but you must understand we have nothing to do with this particular situation. I can only tell you what we... I know. But I can offer you no assistance, regrettably. Please understand, Stony that if we interfere in this situation it could lead to much violence, which could seriously interfere with our present operations."

"I think I get your meaning, Joey, even though you're talking like a Denver lawyer. Why don't you just spell it out for me?"

Joey looked at Som-Marie. "I intend no offense, but this is a very private matter."

"It's alright Joey. She works with me now." Stony figured that should avoid any further explanations. Som-Marie nodded gravely.

"Then I will proceed. Again, I am sorry we cannot offer you any assistance," beckoning them to chairs, he half sat on a desk, "There is a Thai criminal gang who's headquarters is in a village just south of Bangkok. We have been successful in keeping them out of our business affairs here in Bangkok, if you understand."

Stony nodded, "I understand."

Joey continued, "They resent us very much, which is why we must avoid giving them any reason to renew open hostilities. Since we have closed certain avenues to them, they have resorted to controlling the narcotics trade in this area. That is not an interest of ours. This trade includes the local American military. That is the general situation, but is only background for why I requested you here tonight. We have learned that this gang is presently holding an American prisoner."

Stony and Som-Marie exchanged glances. "We would be interested in any information you could give us, of course. Especially specific directions to these guys and anything about the prisoner," said Stony.

"About the prisoner, we know nothing, except that he is an American who has been living in Bangkok. About these criminals, we know much, because it is our self interest to do so. There are three men, who are in charge, but not all of them are in the village at any time. Some are out supervising their underlings. They are always protected by a group of tough guys, young punks with guns. The villagers are all afraid of them. We know the village very well. Here, I can draw you a map." Which he proceeded to do. "There is one

177

more thing. The mother of the village leader died some time ago. Tomorrow night there will be a cremation of her accompanied by a village celebration. It might give you an opportunity to act."

"Opportunity or not, we're going in. Thank Joey."

"Would you and your lady wish to join me for drinks?"

"Thank you, no. It's been a long day and tomorrow will likely be a tough one. We'd better be going. Thank you again." They shook hands and Stony and Som-Marie made their way through the packed club, out to the little brown car and back to the ambassador's compound. At the house, Stony called JJ, who had just arrived home himself.

"Glad I got you, JJ. I might have found out where Allan is being held."

"What have you got?"

"I don't understand the connection, but a gang of Thai dope pushers has an American prisoner in a village just south of Bangkok."

"Meet me at the office and we'll raid the bastards."

"Whoa up, 'ol buddy. I've also found out that there will be some kind of celebration in the village tomorrow night. How about we get some shut-eye and plan this in the morning?"

"Sounds good. I'm half in the bag anyhow."

CHAPTER 10

Stony and Som-Marie weren't finished with breakfast when they began arriving. JJ had picked up Richard from his hotel. JJ looked to be in good shape but Richard was obviously suffering from a short night's sleep.

"Look at him, Stony. I don't know how he does it. I'm more than somewhat fatigued but he looks totally refreshed."

"It's just a little trick I learned early in this business where you catch sleep when you can," answered JJ.

"And what is that. May I ask?"

"Simple. I just sleep fast," he grinned as he took a drink of his coffee.

Richard just rolled his eyes as he held out his hand to receive the coffee offered by Stony. Pete and John ambled in and went straight for the coffee, silently.

"I called everybody just before I hit the rack," said JJ to Stony's unasked question. "We're gonna need your lady's input on this, so I figured we could meet here just as well as in the conference room over in the embassy. Richard agreed."

"To start things out," JJ continued, "I drew a blank on the bar circuit last night. Stopped by the embassy on our way over and put in a call to our Chinat contact. Didn't tell him much, but enough to get them to start looking. How about you guys?"

"Spent half the night getting our people working on it, but nobody knew anything up front. Maybe they'll have something later, if Stony's lead doesn't pan out," said Pete. "What do you have Stony?"

"Could be what we're looking for, I don't know. Allan had his faults but I don't think he ever got close to narcotics," answered Stony, "unless, maybe it was through his kitoy."

"His what?" asked Richard.

"Kitoy," answered JJ, "female impersonator. Not uncommon here in Bangkok. Stony and I found Allan and his Kitoy tangled together like two dogs in heat in a bar over on Patpong Road last week. I thought I would yank his chain by sending over a drink. The bartender's the one who told us it was a kitoy and said they were in there pretty often."

"That's hard to believe. He's been with us for years," said Richard as he stood up and paced a little, rubbing his jaw. "Are you absolutely certain?"

"We're certain," answered Stony. "In his defense, it's not easy to tell the difference. Some kitoys can pass for very good looking women." He glanced at Som-Marie, who closed her eyes and nodded affirmatively. Richard sat down heavily at the table again.

"This is rapidly becoming more than a brush fire, gentlemen."

Stony figured it would be a good idea to change conversational directions. "I've got a map to the village. There is going to be some kind of funeral celebration there this evening. Som-Marie can explain it better than I can."

"It is a little complicated, bit I will try." She began, "A Thai funeral is not the somber affair that it is in your culture. Many Thai's, especially those at the village level, believe in reincarnation and hope to reappear in a better life. Also, the body is often kept in a tight coffin in the family house for up to a year after the death. It is kept decorated with flowers and incense is burned to propitiate the dead person's spirit. Family and friends will come to offer homage and to burn incense, not only out of respect but to keep the dead one's spirit from tormenting them for not giving it a proper send off. There is often a lot of Animism mixed with Buddhism in this country." She looked around at each of them, measuring their comprehension. "That is the background. As far as tonight is concerned, since this woman was the mother of the village's mayor, and because he is fairly well off, there will be a great funeral pyre built with her coffin placed on top of it. There will be fireworks and a carnival, at least, to entertain the villagers and guests. Later at midnight, they will light the funeral pyre. There will be much excitement and commotion in the village which will help to cover our movements."

"Thank you Som-Marie. That was very interesting. I did note one curious term you used just at the end. I believe you referred to 'our movements' did you not?" asked Richard as he turned questioningly to Stony.

Som-Marie smiled and said, "I appreciate your concern, Richard, but you will need me during this mission, if I may call it that, unless one of you can speak Thai. And by the way, I hold a black belt in two disciplines of the Marital Arts."

"Just when you think you know somebody," grinned Stony.

Pete pushed his chair back and laughed, "Hell, Som-Marie, we're sending you to get Allan," he made a sweeping gesture with his arm, indicating the rest of the group, "we're just gonna watch."

"Ah, levity. It is always good to employ a little levity to relieve a serious moment," said Richard, "but tell me, Som-Marie, what disciplines do you possess your black belts in?"

"Judo and Karate. I was introduced to Judo by a friend and enjoyed it as a hobby. After gaining my black belt, I began training in Karate. I am an occasional instructor at the Bangkok Sports Club."

"Man, that would be real embarrassing, I mean me being taken out by a little girl like you," chided John.

Stony laid the hastily drawn map he had received from Joey Li on the table. It didn't show much, but it did follow the canal that paralleled the New Phetburi Road out past Bangkapi towards the targeted village. The village itself was only a circle on the map but Joey had marked two small piers, noting that one was just this side of the village.

"I suggest," said Stony, running his finger along the marked canals, "that we take the klong – that's what they call the canals here, Richard - that way we can get right into the village before we are noticed. We can get a couple of long-tailed boats and arrive well after dark, just like we're part of the funeral gathering."

"Long-tailed boats?" asked Richard.

"Yea. It's the most common of personal transportation on the water around here. Just a long, shallow canoe powered by a four cylinder car engine that runs a long shaft to a propeller," offered JJ, "The engine pivots to accommodate depth and vegetation conditions. The long tail shaft it gives the name."

"We'd better call the professor on this," said Pete, "we'll have to rent the boats; no drivers are going to want to be part of hitting these guys."

"We wouldn't want any witnesses anyway," added John, "but without local drivers we're going to have to travel most of the way by daylight."

"That could pose a problem. There may be a lot of people taking the klongs and a bunch of foreigners loitering in one spot is bound to draw attention," said JJ, "let me work on that."

Richard pushed back his chair and walked around the table, crouching beside Som-Marie.

"Have you thought this out, Som-Marie? We are foreigners going up against your people. This isn't law enforcement action; the other side has no rights. This is a military style raid. The only factors we will consider are the accomplishment of our mission and the safety of our team members."

"I understand this, Richard, but this is not a question of nationality. This is strictly a situation in which a kidnap victim is rescued. Also, I have seen what narcotics can do to otherwise good people and I have no sympathy for narcotics dealers. If you want my help in this, then you have it, one hundred percent."

Stony reached over, putting his hand on hers, and she turned her palm up to hold onto his, "One more thing, Som-Marie, you should consider what could happen if we lose."

She put on her most reassuring face, "I intend to be right in the middle of this, Stony. You can only lose by being killed, and if so, I die with you." She raised her shoulders in a shrug.

Stony's eyebrows rose at her candor. If she fooled everyone else, she didn't fool him. She gripped his hand so hard that her nails bit into his flesh.

The meeting broke up with everyone off to make his share of preparations. Stony, JJ and Richard to the embassy, Pete and John to reconnoiter and later to meet the professor about JJ's arranged boats. Som-Marie went shopping for black sweats, black scarves, and three large white windbreakers.

At the office, JJ persuaded the professor to include one trusted driver, for a fat fee, and to have two boats at a dock behind the Happy OK Motel on Phetburi Road. It was just a hooker hotel but it would provide a parking lot and a dark boarding area. They cleaned weapons taken from the office locker.

At ten minutes before nine that night, a long-tailed boat, with another in tow pulled up to the concrete steps that lead down from the wall to the canal. Six individuals in dark clothes and temporarily dark-tanned faces eased from two small cars. Som-Marie quietly asked the driver if he was the one to take them to the little village of Ban Prasat, only a few kilometers past the Navy golf course near Bangkapi. He was. Stony, JJ and Som-Marie boarded the second boat, Richard, Pete and John in the lead with the driver. JJ had dropped a duffel bag into each boat. Each bag contained two fragmentation grenades and Winchester model 1200 Defender shot guns. Black, pistol-gripped, 18 inch barrels with a seven shot magazine, no sights to snag, for each male team member. Som-Marie had declined to be armed. Loaded with 12-guage 'double-aught' buckshot, the Defender was the closest thing you could get to personal artillery for close-in fighting. The lead boat's bag also contained the three white windbreakers with black armbands.

JJ fired up the second boat's engine and together they eased into mid-channel. The only illumination was the usual small, not too bright, kerosene lantern hanging from a pole mounted on the prow of each small boat. The trip took just over an hour with two klong changes. The going was slow as the driver cautiously cruised his way past small fragile boat docks and the boats tied to them. The klong was not more than forty feet wide and oncoming boats passed near enough to speak, which some did. Som-Marie and the driver politely answered back. The enveloping blackness was only relieved by the lanterns of the occasional other boats and the starlight that formed its own channel above them between the overhanging trees.

Traffic picked up some as they neared the village, but in the dark they were hardly noticed. Som-Marie took Stony's hand several times and he could sense her excitement. He reached up and squeezed her shoulders as a measure of reassurance once in a while.

According to plan, Stony's boat stopped at the dock while Pete and company continued to the main pier. Joey had said the gang's place was about midway between the two, on the outskirts of the village. Pete, John and Richard were to don matching, loose fitting, white windbreakers, under which they were to hide their short shotguns. The idea was to be noticed and hopefully flush out the gang members, sending them back to their hideout in a defensive maneuver, to be intercepted by Stony's team.

Etiquette for guests at a Thai cremation ceremony demanded black dress for women and white attire for men, with a black armband. Foreigners wearing white jackets with black armbands over black trousers would not necessarily alarm the tolerant Thai's, but with an American prisoner, the gang members would definitely take notice.

JJ eased the boat towards the shaky dock, which was really only a plank tied to small poles anchored in the mud. As soon as he could, Stony grabbed a pole and JJ killed the engine. They hooked grenades into their belts, shoved extra shells in their pockets and grabbed the Defenders. Som-Marie roped the boat to the dock and untied the lantern from its stick. Stony helped her onto the dock. The lantern would barely light the way without illuminating themselves unnecessarily. Stony hoped the cobras and pythons were busy elsewhere. They could see almost nothing outside the shallow circle of lantern glow, but could feel the oppressive jungle about them.

As they made their way toward the darkened village, they could hear the music and occasional fireworks. They entered the village and chose a narrow lane paralleling the klong. The gang's place was supposed to be on the outskirts. The lights of the carnival on the other side of the village somewhat illuminated the huts and houses as they snaked through the deserted back streets. The homes were mainly stucco'd concrete block and wood, with metal or thatched roofs, all the inhabitants of which were evidently at the festivities.

At one point, noticing the absence of a roof, Stony handed his defender to Som-Marie and eased himself up to look over the wall. Bingo! There were three guards strolling the grounds with holstered pistols on their belts. The walled compound contained a main house set towards the rear and several small buildings, all stucco with corrugated metal roofs. The only outside light was a bare bulb hanging from a tall pole. They silently scouted the perimeter. There was a vehicle-wide gate up front in the middle of a high stone wall and two small, locked gates in the back. The house was two-story with some windows shuttered but with weak electric lights in most of the rooms. They could find no other guards. With no evidence of big money about, Stony concluded that for dope pushers they didn't seem to be making much income from it. His opinion of the gang declined precipitously.

One small building against the west side wall was flat-topped with a two foot high wall around the top. Probably for collecting rain water, but it was dry at the moment. They quickly, but quietly climbed into it and waited.

It wasn't a long wait. One side of the main gate flew open and three Thai men ran through, the last one casting a quick look backwards just before he latched it. They said something to one of the guards, who ran into the house.

"He's checking on the prisoner," Som-Marie whispered, "they are alarmed about your men."

"Good news. That means things are going according to plan. It shouldn't be long now."

Stony could see the guard pass briefly by one of the open windows upstairs. That narrowed the prisoner's room down to one of the two shuttered windows up there, he figured. The three new guys pulled automatic pistols from their belts and joined the other two as they climbed on chairs and boxes to peer warily over the wall.

"If our guys noticed these men leaving the area they won't have much trouble tracking them. This is the only lit up place outside the village center," said JJ in a hushed tone.

"JJ, there are five outside and one in the house. We need to somehow get them all together."

"Not in the house, if that's what you're thinking. Wait. Something's going on out front."

The men at the wall jumped down and were chattering in whispers as they formed a semi-circle and trained their weapons on the main gate. After a few minutes the latch slowly lifted and one side of the gate opened inward just slightly. Suddenly a masked figure in a white jacket darted in. The edgy gunmen all opened fire at once, cutting him down in his tracks. A grenade tossed from over the wall exploded behind the gunmen just as two more dark figures topped the wall, their shotguns barking rapidly. Stony and JJ each pitched a grenade into the gang and leaped from their rooftop hideaway, firing and pumping as the hail of fire and grenades reduced the gunmen to a group of sprawling, motionless bodies.

Gunfire erupted above and behind Stony. He felt something slam into his right side. It spun him around and threw him to the ground. Instinctively he yanked out his 38 and began to fire at the open second floor balcony door. Every other member of the team had already begun firing at the same target. Windows shattered and the force slammed the door shut again. They stopped firing. All was quiet. With great effort, Stony sat up and checked his side, just above the belt, pulling back a blood-soaked hand. JJ rushed over and helped him to his feet. They all began to cautiously rush the house. Waves of pain were erupting from Stony's side as he fought to retain consciousness.

A great commotion came from the upstairs room. Suddenly a man crashed through the double balcony doors, glass and wood exploding from the force. His body lurched over the iron railing and slammed hard onto the ground below. One leg and his neck were obviously broken.

With pain streaking through his upper body, Stony forced himself forward. JJ was just ahead of him and kicked in the front door as another body tumbled down the stairs and landed at their feet. JJ swept the room with his Defender and seeing no one, reached down and felt the gunman's neck for a pulse. He was still alive, barely.

At the top of the stairway appeared Som-Marie. When she caught sight of Stony, she raced down the steps and hugged him tightly. It hurt, but it hurt good.

"I saw him shoot you, I saw you fall down, I thought you were dead!" She looked down; saw the bloody shirt and trousers. Weakened by the loss of blood, Stony stumbled slightly. Quickly, with JJ's help, she sat him on a step.

"Did… did you do all that?" he asked as Richard, Pete and John came running in.

"You're prisoner is upstairs, alone," she said to them as they headed up the stairs. She ran to a back room and returned with some rags and a wet cloth with which she began wiping Stony's forehead. She pulled away his shirt with its matted and oozing blood and cleaned at the wound the best she could.

"This is very unsanitary, but it looks like it went clear through." She made a compress from the rags and bound his side tightly. "We must get you to a doctor."

"I'm alright, sweetheart," he protested, "But you could have been killed. How did you get up there anyway?"

"Well, when you and JJ jumped from the front of the roof, I dropped from the side and slipped into the house. I knew the man in the house would shoot at you, so I tried to stop him. I was too late. He shot you and through an open window, I saw you fall. I hid when you all began firing but when it stopped, he was going to shoot again. I was furious because I thought he had killed you. Is he…"

"Broke his neck when he took his swan dive off the balcony. But this one is alive. By the way, I heard all the commotion in that room up there. I hope I never have to see you 'furious' again."

"There were *two* men in the house; one was in with the prisoner. He attacked me just after I had finished with the other one, but he is slow."

JJ laughed, "Slowed right down to a stop, now."

"Sorry, boys, close but no cigar." It was John. He and Pete were holding a man at the top of the stairs. With great effort Stony turned to look up. The man was rather short and pudgy, wearing a light green pullover t-shirt and rumpled green slacks. A loose canvas bag was over his head, which Pete yanked off with a flourish. The man, about thirty, with dirty blond, close cropped hair, blinked in the light. His hands remained tied behind his back.

"Who the hell is this?" questioned JJ.

"Our kidnap victim," offered Richard, as he descended the stairs, "Sergeant Otis Crumb, U.S. Air Force, at least for now. Seems he had been selling to other military types for these guys and had been holding out on them. They were probably just teaching him a lesson or he would have been dead by now."

"Better get up, Stony, we're gonna pitch this dirt bag down the stairs," said John, winking.

"No! Please! Don't!" yelled the dirt bag.

"Shaddup, asshole!" said Pete as they half dragged him to the first floor. "This fat little bastard may swamp our boat on the way back, JJ. What are we going to do with him?"

"You could throw a rope around him and troll for cobras." Everybody grinned but the prisoner.

"Seven men died because of this slime bag," said Pete, "if they hadn't been dopers, it would've been a hell of a waste."

"I'd shoot a doper for shits and grins," said John.

"By the way, John," asked JJ, "who was the target that you shoved through the gate?"

"Well, when we noticed the three take off in this direction, we went after them. After we ditched the white jackets, we found that guy following us. We sort of snagged him and my calculating mind saw him as the diversion we would need. I ran back and grabbed one of the jackets and put it on him. We made a gag and mask out of our arm bands. Worked out pretty good, didn't it?"

"Congratulations John. Now how about you and Pete go find that boat driver while Richard and I help Stony get out of here."

"We told him to enjoy himself and we would see him later, Hope we can find him, JJ."

"I'll go," said Som-Marie, "we don't know how much the villagers may have heard of this commotion and I will be less noticeable. We will meet you at the boat dock we used earlier." JJ pitched her one of the flashlights he had found. She kissed Stony on the cheek and left.

"Looks like they have their village back. They can draw their own conclusions when they discover the carnage in the morning," said Richard as he switched off the power to the compound, "I doubt the remaining members will want to resurrect this outfit."

With JJ and Richard assisting Stony, and Pete and John roughly escorting the airman, they backtracked to the dock. John threw the beam of the flashlight in an arc at the jungle around them, briefly catching a pair of yellow eyes. "Take a chance, slime ball. You can run off now and we won't chase you."

"Bullshit! You guys stay close to me, you hear?"

Within minutes of arriving at the dock, they heard the other boat approaching. Som-Marie joined Stony, JJ and Richard in the second boat, with the prisoner, Pete, John and the driver in the other.

"There is a lot of noise at the celebration," she said into Stony's ear, "they have a carnival, an outdoor movie, music and fireworks. The driver said they couldn't hear anything from our direction."

The return trip seemed agonizingly long to Stony, the pain growing by the minute. Som-Marie never let go of his good arm, evidently afraid he might pass out and fall from the boat. JJ turned around to become a backrest, probably for the same reason, Stony surmised.

Stiffness did set in and when he tried to exit at the end of the trip, he needed help. While Pete and John took the prisoner to US MACTHAI Headquarters for charges, which they intended to press personally, if necessary, the rest took Stony to the American Medical Unit, just half a mile up Petchburi Road from their arrival point.

The doctors were courteous and efficient and Richard was able to prevent notification of the authorities, Thai and American, as required for a gunshot wound.

The last thing Stony remembered was JJ standing at the foot of the bed, smiling and speaking without sound as he drifted off.

CHAPTER 11

He awoke to a room flooded with light, way too bright, and he sensed someone's presence. As things gradually came into focus, he squinted at the brilliant hospital room, sunlight flooding through the big glass windows. He was covered only with a sheet. He lifted it and saw the large bandage on his right side. Looking down on his left side, he could see his raven-haired love, her head resting on his bed, sound asleep. She must have been sitting there all along. He raised his hand and gently ran his fingers through her hair. Instantly she sat up, took his hand in hers and kissed it for a long moment. She moved closer, kissed him on the lips. He pulled her towards him and with his good arm, just held her for awhile.

The door opened. It was Richard, smiling.

"Ah, my fearsome twosome. How do you feel, trooper?"

"Sore and stiff, and lying in this bed will only encourage them both. What time is it?"

Richard glanced at his watch. "Four-thirty on the nose."

"We've lost a whole day. Somebody get me some clothes and let's get out of here."

"Sorry 'ol buddy. Even though that's a clean wound, the doctor wants to keep you here for a couple days and then start some therapy."

"I stay here a couple more days, I'll need therapy." He sat up on the side of the bed, slowly and stiffly.

"Well, Mrs. McGraw, what are we going to do with this guy?"

Stony looked at them both and frowned, "Mrs. McGraw?"

Richard laughed, "She wasn't going to leave your side, so I told them she was your wife. They'd never have allowed her to stay otherwise."

Stony noticed she was still in her black sweat suit. He began to feel his throat tighten and his eyes began to water. He grabbed the sheet and slid off the bed to his feet. "So far, so good."

"Just a minute, tough guy." Richard stepped out the door and back in again. He threw a plastic bag onto the bed.

"Like to be prepared. I knew a blockhead like you wouldn't listen to the doctors. There are clothes in there and a small bag of your personals. We took everything off you when you were checked in. By the way, do you always carry a pistol in your boot?"

"Just a little insurance, Richard. I, too, like to be prepared."

Richard smiled, "Well, hurry up and I'll go distract the nurses."

With Som-Marie's help, he dressed as quickly as he could. She opened the door and looked around. All clear. They made it to the elevator, took it to the ground floor and walked out into the sunbathed parking lot. The stifling heat, after the cool inside of the medical unit caused Stony to lean against the shadow side of a car as they waited for Richard. He soon showed and led them to Stony's loaner.

"Richard, this car is so inconspicuous I didn't even notice it myself." Richard drove them back to their temporary lodgings at the ambassador's residence.

While Stony walked around the room, moving what he could to loosen some of the soreness, Richard poured a bourbon and water. Som-Marie went straight to the shower.

"That is some brave woman you have there, Stony. And smart. And beautiful."

"Careful, Richard, I could start to get jealous."

"I am a happily married man my friend," he took a sip of his drink, "But if I weren't... Sorry, you've probably got your own inner conflicts to deal with on this, I imagine."

"You imagine right, Richard. It is complicated from at least a dozen angles." He was doing abbreviated deep knee bends, holding onto a chair.

"I don't envy your dilemma. You've got a real tiger by the tail, my friend. She is every man's dream."

"Seems like I've heard that somewhere before."

"By the way, the boys are taking me to the Oriental for dinner. You are certainly welcome to join us, if you feel you are up to it." He downed the last of his drink.

"Thanks, but I'll pass on this one. I'm a little weaker than I thought. Besides, I've probably been shot so full of antibiotics, I shouldn't drink much. We'll probably just order in tonight."

"Suit yourself. I'm heading to the embassy; we're supposed to meet there. They've been checking their leads. See you in the morning."

"Thanks Richard." And with that, he headed into the bedroom, stripped down with some effort and crawled under the sheet.

"I could have spent all evening under that shower, it felt so good," she said, toweling her hair dry. But he didn't hear her, he was already sound asleep. She closed the bedroom door, finished drying her hair, standing beside the bed and smiling down at the slumbering man she had fallen in love with. She crawled naked into the bed and snuggled up to his left side. Within seconds the accumulated fatigue carried her too, off to sleep.

Sometime after eight that night, Stony awoke. He thought he had heard a quiet sob. Turning his head on the pillow he saw her in the semi-darkness, laying on her back, her eyes moist, and her face wet with tears. He brought his left arm up to her pillow, she lifted her head slightly, and he slid his arm under her and pulled her to him, gently stroking her back. He pulled up a corner of the sheet and began patting her face dry. He kissed her softly. He didn't have to ask her what was wrong as she began to explain.

"I'm sorry. I guess I just think too much. I've never been in love before and I am so in love with you. It's wonderful, but so painful because I know I'll end up losing you." She trembled as she spoke, trying to choke back sobs.

"I've never been so careless before. I've held nothing back, just let myself be completely absorbed in you. It feels so good and yet it hurts so badly." She couldn't talk anymore. He pulled her tight, groping desperately for some way to soothe her. It hurt to see her so sad.

"Remember, sweetheart, that night at the Chinese restaurant when I said we had been given a gift?" He was having trouble speaking with the large lump in his own throat. "And do you remember we decided to accept this gift and let it take us wherever it would? I knew that night I was falling in love with you."

She raised her head and looked at him through her teary eyes, "You did?"

"Absolutely. I'll bet that you were already beginning to fall in love with me."

"Passionately."

"Tell you what. Let's agree not to look too far into the future, say maybe not past this summer."

"This summer? Why this summer?"

"Because we've got to face it, one way or another time is running out on my stay in your wonderful country. I'll have to return home to the kids and the ranch and you'll have to finish your semester at the university. But then, I want you to spend the summer on the ranch with me."

"Really? You do?"

"You bet. And if I'm lucky you'll fall in love with Colorado and never want to leave me again. You know, I've got a beautiful little paint gelding that you could ride."

She lifted her head again, "What is a paint gelding?"

"An Indian pony, with splotches of brown and white all over him." He could feel her spirits picking up. Their parting was more remote now. A short separation followed by a reunion. Life looked a little brighter for her, he figured.

"I've never ridden a horse before. Is it difficult?"

"Nothing to it. Especially with Little Duke. Plumb gentle. He was well broke when I bought him, let's see now… He was a three year old, I bought him when Clancy was just walking and he's fifteen, so the pony's about eighteen years old now. The kids grew up with him. Even saw Rose Ann napping on his back once or twice while he was grazing. I'll buy you some western outfits. Western clothes always look so good on the ladies, but in your case, I'd say you'll be doing them a favor in return."

"And a hat. I've always wanted a cowboy hat." She was definitely feeling much better.

"Of course a hat. No decent cowgirl would be caught riding without her hat. Maybe we'll even get you a lariat." He grinned at her, "Maybe then I'll put you to work." His hand slipped down to her firm, soft bottom. She couldn't help but notice his reaction.

"I thought you were feeling weak."

"Not that weak."

"Well, since you have been wounded, you just lay here and enjoy yourself. I will take care of everything." And she did. Throwing the sheet off them, she straddled him. She leaned forward smiling, her long dark hair falling across her firm, bronze breasts; their creamy brown nipples peeking tempting through. Soon, she was rocking slowly, gently. His hands rested on her rising and falling thighs. It felt good, so very good. After awhile, she began to breathe heavily, and she began to moan quietly. He felt her quivering and then his own stomach tightened involuntarily. He tightened his grip on her legs, pulling her down on him, thrusting, grinding, exploding, and then the passion spent itself.

They kissed and she laid bedside him, her head on his chest as he gently stroked her hair. They cat-napped a few minutes and she left the room. When she returned, dressed in a light belted robe, she helped him from the bed, wrapped a towel around his middle and led him to the dining room table. She had it covered with sheets and indicated he should climb up on it. With her help, he did.

"You need a good massage." She began to work over his chest and back thoroughly with her skilled hands. It felt better to him than weeks of therapy possibly could have. Afterward, she helped him bathe.

"How do you feel now?"

"Great! Absolutely great! You have magic in those pretty, little hands. In fact, I feel so good, I'm starving."

"It's after ten, too late to call on the servants to cook. Maybe I could prepare something over in the common kitchen."

He began pulling on a shirt. "I've got a better idea. Let's go to the Intercon for a big juicy steak. My treat." He could see the look of concern on her face, but she agreed.

They parked deep in the parking lot, sat there a few minutes to see if they had been followed, but then strolled hand in hand into the restaurant. It wasn't too late in this night owl city for a good dinner out. He skipped the aperitif and the bottle of Bordeaux, but since he was having prime rib, he did have a glass of house burgundy. Som-Marie decided on the same, with a green salad.

"Surprised?" she asked.

"I didn't realize you were so hungry."

"These past few days have been very strenuous. I need my nutritional batteries recharged."

"Well you certainly charged my batteries this evening. I can't believe how good I feel. And you. You look great. In fact, you've never looked prettier than you do right now." She demurely smiled.

They were enjoying themselves. The stress of yesterday had melted away and they felt a temporary freedom from the problems lurking just out of sight. The dinner was excellent, as usual, and as they were slowly walking back to the car, arm in arm, Stony made a suggestion. He glanced at his watch. It was 11:50.

"It's a little over an hour before they close, let's go to the Derby for just a few minutes."

"You really are taking chances tonight, aren't you?"

"We deserve it. What are they gonna do, shoot me?" he laughed.

The band was taking its last break for the night, so it was fairly quiet as they entered the club. Joey Li was seated at the corner of the bar; Stony patted his back as they passed by.

"Nice job."

"One less competitor. Ought to be worth a drink or two."

"At least. You OK?"

"Just a scratch. Never better." He winked as they headed for a back table, the same one she had been sitting at the night he met her.

"Isn't this romantic? Did you know that no one has been allowed to sit at this table since that night?"

She giggled, "Sure."

He ordered a gin and tonic for her, an Amarit beer for himself, which he nursed until they left. The waiter said it was on the house. The band began to play a rock'n roll fast tune but followed it with a slow dance, another staple, "Detroit City." As soon as the tempo slowed, he asked her to join him on the dance floor. He was still somewhat in pain, so they just held each other close and swayed to the music. He spotted the Burmese guy also on the dance floor, with the tiger lady mounted on his left leg. Her dancing should be x-rated, he thought. Seductive as she was, he only had eyes for Som-Marie this night. In fact, he didn't believe she could hold a candle to the enchanting lady he held in his own arms just now.

He felt an elbow nudge him. It was the Burmese. He wasn't smiling.

"I must speak to you tonight. It is very urgent," he looked at Som-Marie, and then back to Stony, "alone, you must be totally alone."

"Alright, let's talk."

"Not here. Later. Meet me in front of the Erawam Hotel on Rajadamri Road, one o'clock."

"Not much time to take our ladies home."

"I will wait for you. It is very important."

With that, the Burmese turned and left the floor. He dropped some money on their table and exited the club. Stony and Som-Marie finished the dance and returned to their table. Somber-faced, she finished her drink, Stony left half his beer. She didn't want him to go to this meeting, sensing some unknown danger. Stony knew he had to go although he was in no shape for a fight, especially with this guy. He wished he had some backup on this one but his men were out with Richard tonight. Might blow things anyway.

He took her back to the house at the ambassador's place.

"Whatever happens, you'll be safest here. Now don't worry, he probably just wants to talk. Back soon." He kissed her and left. Retracing his route up Wittayu Road, left on Ploenchit and left on Rajadamri into the parking lot of the aging but still eloquent, Erawan Hotel. The Burmese was already there. He walked quickly to Stony's car and looked at it strangely.

"Loaner," Stony informed him.

Maung shook his head gravely, "Follow my car."

He led Stony further down Rajadamri Road, turned down a side street and pulled up near a gate to Lumphini Park. This is Bangkok's version of central park with large close-cropped lawns, wooded areas and a huge lake in the middle, on one side of which was a fancy floating restaurant. Stony remembered reading that the park was named after the Buddha's birthplace in Nepal, or something like that. The main walkways were lighted, albeit inadequately. At this time of night, after one A.M. it was deserted. Like any big city park at night, it wasn't a secure place to be. Stony figured he had better be ready for anything. He had checked his 38 and adjusted his boot pistol. He decided he wasn't capable of duking it out with this guy, not tonight anyway, so at the first sign of trouble he would simply shoot the bastard. If anyone joined them, they would do it at the end of his barrel.

Maung got out of his car, motioning Stony to follow as he entered the park through an open gate. Cautious, Stony followed although the big man was in a hurry. The pace was difficult for Stony. Maung had chosen a dimly lit area for his stroll. Eventually, they stopped at a bench in a clearing. Each looked around, although apparently for different reasons. When Maung was sure they were alone, he silently beckoned Stony to sit with him. The sounds of city traffic were distant now, the air had cooled comfortably, and Stony could appreciate the relatively clean air provided by the surrounding vegetation. Although he tried to appear casual, Stony's every muscle was wired to spring into action. It proved to be unnecessary.

"Mister McGraw, you must be exceedingly curious as to why I have brought you to this particular place. For our business tonight, believe me, it is the best possible location. First, please apologize for me to your lady friend, I meant no offense to her, but as you will see, I can take no chances about what I will tell you. I am about to reveal something to you that could be very dangerous for me if my own government learned of it. I must ask for your complete secrecy about what I will tell you. May I have it?"

Stony was becoming more curious than alarmed, and more than a little impatient. "You're going a long way around the bar, but yes, I give you my word about you as a source. You realize though, that if this is some information I… we, can use, we will have to act on it."

"Precisely." Maung looked around again, and then he turned to Stony, and began gravely, "I am a man of honor, sir, and I owe you something and so I will pay my debt. I will tell you three things and on my honor they are true. First, and the most sensitive, I am a secret agent for my government; the ex-im business is merely a cover. I could be executed for revealing that to you. But it will explain why I know and can tell you the next two things."

"Whoa, hoss. I kinda suspected that. Can you expand on that a little?"

Maung looked nervously about. Although he was barely visible in the darkness, Stony figured he was sweating profusely under his huge Madras shirt.

Maung shrugged, "What more harm can I do to myself? Alright. It is simply this. Before our government embraced socialism, the gemstone mines, which are extensive in Burma, were in private enterprise, with many gem mines, all making a nice profit. However, under socialism the mines were nationalized and the income of the freelance miners was severely reduced. Their reaction was to initiate an extensive smuggling operation, especially to Bangkok. I have been working for two and a half years on this problem. We have several agents dedicated to this activity."

Stony smiled, "And the tiger lady is one of them?"

Maung looked at him quizzically but otherwise ignored the comment. He continued, "We are making real progress against the smugglers until just over a year ago when we suffered an unfortunate setback through the collusion of a foreign intelligence agent and the remnants of the Chinese Nationalist Army." He leaned into Stony's face. "We are sure it was an American, incidentally."

Stony struggled to suppress a grin. "Go on."

"That is all I can tell you about that, except that I have cultivated many informants, over time. Therefore, I am prepared to tell you this. I am aware of what happened to your wife something over a year ago."

The hair on Stony's neck stiffened. His eyes hardened but with effort he remained outwardly calm. "What exactly do you know?"

"Not much really. Only what has been reported and this. I understand that my leaving Bangkok about that time propelled me to a primary position on the list of suspects, at least to certain people. I assure you sir, on my word of honor that I had absolutely nothing to do with that. I can only hope you believe me. I can offer no proof of my innocence except that you may check the records that will show you that my father did die at that time and I was in Mandalay taking care of the arrangements. If you wish, I can provide you with the necessary information that will enable you to verify this."

Stony stood, took a few steps away. This did jive with what Wirey had told him earlier and if it wasn't true, why would he bring it up and lay himself open like this? He decided to believe him, even though it hit him like another body blow. He turned back to Maung.

"Not necessary. It sure sets me back to square one, but I guess I'll just have to accept that. Is this why you wanted to talk to me tonight? You did say there was a third thing." He sat back down again.

Maung put out his massive hand, Stony shook it.

"Thank you. Your trust in the matter means a great deal to me. By the way, how is the man doing that was wounded last night?"

Stony frowned and stared intently at Maung.

"Don't be so surprised, Mister McGraw. Intelligence work of different nations does overlap occasionally. The man you didn't kill was one of my informants. In fact, he is part of the reason we are meeting tonight. Your efficient raid solved many problems, including one of yours. I understand you are missing one of your men. The man you found last night was not who you were looking for. Am I right?"

"You've thrown a wide loop, Maung. Hope you can hold onto everything that it settles on. And yes, we are still missing one of our men. Do you know something?"

Maung leaned back against the armrest of the bench. "I know where he is."

"Are you sure it is our man. We don't need another wild goose chase."

"Reasonably sure. I will describe him. He is bald-headed, short and overweight. He is a chain smoker and there is a Thai woman with him. I believe she must be a prostitute."

"Close enough. Anything else?"

"The people who live in the area are not Thai, but came across the border from Burma. They are tolerated but not liked by the Thais. I have friends among them. Your man is in a house near a set of caves northwest of Ratburi. You should have no trouble finding the caves; in one of them is a statue of the reclining Buddha. It is a popular shrine. I don't know your man's condition or why he is there. I understand you have reason to believe he has been kidnapped."

"We have a note, and then why else would he be in a place like that. He could have taken a prostitute to almost any resort."

"You have a point. Now I have told you all that I intended and more. Good night. Oh, you didn't tell me the condition of the man who was wounded. Evidently he left a great deal of blood at the scene."

Stony grimaced and raised the right side of his shirt enough to reveal the bandage. Even in the limited light, Stony could see that Maung was visibly startled.

"Why, it hasn't been twenty-four hours! You are an amazing man, Stony.

"That's what all the girls tell me." It was corny but they both laughed.

Stony held out his hand, "Thank you so much, Ba. You are a man of honor in my book."

Som-Marie was still up when he returned, just after two. She rushed over to hug him.

"You sure are a worry-wart."

"Whatever that is, I hope you love it."

"Oh, I do. I do."

"How are you feeling? You look tired."

"I am tired. Been a hell of a day. But I can tell you this. If you liked our last escapade, you're going to love this one."

CHAPTER 12

It seemed his head had hardly hit the pillow when he was jostled awake by the phone. Daylight flooded the room. He glanced at his watch, it was almost eight o'clock. He had been sleeping for over five hours.

"Hey, wake up, ol' buddy," it was JJ, "I thought you cowboys were up before the sun every morning. I'm at the office and it looks like a pretty full day ahead. I'll be over to get you shortly and I'll even spring for breakfast here at the embassy."

"A full day's not half of it, JJ. Put a hold on everything until we talk." He couldn't say anymore over the phone.

Within 15 minutes JJ arrived. They were ready. He took one long look at Som-Marie, "My, my, don't we look professional."

Her hair was pulled into a bun. She was wearing a short-sleeved, light pink blouse over a medium length, rose colored, Thai-silk skirt and black pumps.

She smiled at JJ, "I am Mister McGraw's personal assistant, am I not?"

On the way to the office, Stony told him he thought he might have found Allan for real this time, and it was near to where Som-Marie was raised and that she knew the area.

"Damn, Stony, to hell with breakfast, we should talk about this right now." He turned to Som-Marie, "You know, doll, we should put you on the payroll. You seem to have become a critical member of this team lately."

"Tell you what, JJ, how about just picking up some rolls at the cafeteria and we'll meet you in the conference room. What I really need is a cup of wake up."

Stony and Som-Marie proceeded directly to the 3rd floor conference room, flipping on the red light as they entered. JJ went for rolls and a call into the office brought Pete out carrying the coffee pot, John following with a stack of cups. Everyone took seats around the conference table and JJ notified the group of Stony's new information about Allan as they hit the rolls and coffee. Complications surfaced immediately.

Richard entered somber-faced, and before he sat down, announced, "I'm very sorry to inform you men, but I have been called back to Washington for some sort of emergency, by the Director himself, I might add. Regrettably, I must leave immediately. Sorry, I realize the timing couldn't be worse."

"You ain't the only one baling on this caper, Richard." It was Pete. "The Defense Attaché just handed me tonight's little 'kill 'em' mission to Nam. Says it's already coordinated all down the line - no way out. And I believe it is JJ and Stony's turn." He furrowed his forehead in a look of apologetic regret.

JJ had his cheekbone propped on his fist, dejectedly staring at the table top. He raised his head and slammed his fist down hard on the table.

"Dammit, this calls for a command decision. With your permission, Richard, but I am senior agent here in this office and here is the plan. Nothing we can do about Richard leaving or the mission to Nam tonight, but we *can* decide how we handle things. Sorry, Pete, John, but you're going to have to take the Nam mission. Stony and I, with Som-Marie's help will go after Allan. It's risky but we just can't wait for things to get any better."

"If I may have a moment," interrupted Richard, still standing, "I must admit I haven't felt all that useful here, and I mean that as a compliment. You seem to have every situation well in hand. JJ, I'm placing you temporarily in charge, to make it official. Pete, John, you are doing superb work, keep it up. Stony," he walked over to Som-Marie, took her hand and kissed it, "and you, lovely lady, if you two happen to team up permanently, we could use the both of you in the future. You are a rare and impressive sight together. Oh, by the way, Som-Marie, I did some checking and you are eligible for U.S. citizenship, it's only a matter of paperwork and I could speed things along rather easily. Just a thought." He strode to the door, turned, "There, I've even managed to include an annual evaluation in this short visit. I'll return the paperwork soon. Good luck." He closed the door behind himself. For a long moment, not a word was spoken.

JJ turned to Som-Marie, "Well, you sure impressed the boss. Good for you. Now I have two questions. First, do you intend to accompany us on this mission, and two, could you tell us something about the area?"

She sat pensive for a moment. Stony looked at her questioningly.

"Oh. Sorry. I was just thinking about what Richard just said. To answer your questions, yes, by all means, I intend to accompany you. And about the area, we are talking about a location a little over 100 kilometers from here. It is a very different terrain. I grew up just south of Ratburi; its real name is Ratchaburi, actually. I have visited the place several times with my relatives. There are many caves there but only two are visited by outsiders. One is a long, narrow cave, in which there is a revered statue of the reclining Buddha. It has electricity and is relatively cool. The other is a source of water for the surrounding villagers. They must walk a long ways for water now. The deforestation by the lumber industry is blamed for the perennial drought that has overtaken the land. The cave itself is huge and very hot. The villagers are mostly non-Thai, who have emigrated from nearby Burma and are mainly Karins and some Mons. They do not mix very well with the Thais who tolerate them but still consider them to be foreigners. I learned the rudiments of their languages when I was young, so I can translate for you – at least as well as I can. Oh, and you should try to get a Jeep or other military vehicle. The roads are deeply rutted by the lumber trucks and I don't believe an automobile could traverse them successfully."

JJ stood, "Thanks Som-Marie that gives us something of a picture. John, see if Colonel White can arrange for a Jeep or something. We'll use only the shotguns and pistols. While we don't know the exact location, or just how many are holding Allan, we don't have any choice but to make this raid."

Colonel White did come up with a Jeep, which didn't arrive until just after lunch. Stony and Som-Marie had used the time to go to the house and change clothes and eat. Some-Marie into a tan cotton blouse over brown slacks and tennis shoes, Stony dug into his bag and came up with a light blue, Chambray cotton cowboy shirt and jeans. He left the tail of the shirt out for now to conceal his pistol.

As they approached the Jeep, JJ muttered, "No top. This is going to be one hot trip."

"And also long," offered Som-Marie, "I would estimate it to be about four hours. After we leave the paved roads, the going will be very difficult and slow."

They piled in; JJ driving as usual, Stony rode shotgun and Som-Marie in back sharing space with the canvas bag of weapons and extra water, which she had suggested.

They headed south out of Bangkok, on Sukhumvit Road, then west on the road to Nakhon Pathom. A few kilometers down the road they turned south towards Ratchaburi. After a few minutes in this direction Som-Marie leaned forward between the seats.

"I hate to say this, but I think we are being followed. There are two cars. They are not too close, but they have been back there since we left Nakhon Pathom, maybe since Bangkok, but that highway was too busy to notice them. When we turned south, I watched for them and they followed us."

"My guess is that it could be only one of two groups," said JJ, "part of the kidnappers or your Captain Pibul."

"We have the advantage with this Jeep," said Stony, "we could take some of these side roads and elude them."

"I have an idea," offered Som-Marie, "up ahead there is a small village. We can skirt it on the back roads. When they get to the village they will probably ask if we have been through. When they find out we haven't, they will start searching for us down these dirt side roads. It might provide enough time for us to escape them."

"Good idea, sweetheart. Let's switch seats and you can navigate," said Stony and they clambered into each other's seats. After a few minutes, Som-Marie directed JJ to slow down as she searched for a convenient side road. She selected one and JJ eased the Jeep off to the right side of the road into the weeds, took the corner slowly and stayed in the roadside weeds for another hundred feet.

"Won't be so obvious when they start backtracking that way," he grinned as he leaned over towards Som-Marie conspiratorially. The road was powder dry so JJ drove slowly for a mile or so to cut down on the dust trail. The ride was hot but the open Jeep allowed for enough breeze to make it tolerable. The road was so rough that he had to drive slowly at times and they weren't always ahead of their dust cloud. After a couple of left turns, they again found Highway 4 and continued to Ratchaburi.

"I'd like to skirt this town too, but I read that it has a population of over forty thousand people, that'd be a hell of a detour. Besides, we'd better top up our fuel. Don't know what we'll run into out there. Anyway it might be better to let ourselves be seen in case things go badly and somebody has to come looking for us."

They filled the Jeep and drove around town in various directions so as to be seen and then headed south again, stopping at a side street market to buy some local fruit, as Some-Marie suggested, in order to conserve water. They had been hitting it rather heavily. She called the fruit Sommo and it was sort of grapefruit looking and yielded a thirst quenching liquid. South of town under Som-Marie's direction, they headed west towards the border of Burma.

The vegetation became sparser, with many areas of bare dirt ground. Most of the klongs were dried up. The terrain became hillier, the road more deeply rutted and the passing lumber trucks smothered them with dust. Their perspiration combined with the dust and soon they were feeling very uncomfortable, especially Stony. The bouncing and sweating had started his side throbbing. The movement of the bandage had also opened his wound some. Once when he slipped his left hand over it, hoping not to be noticed by the others, he could tell it was leaking a little blood. He said nothing. Although he knew Som-Marie was keeping a worried eye on him, and he suspected she was aware of his latest difficulty, she kept it to herself. The conditions made progress slow. Occasionally they passed oxen pulling simple carts and women with long poles over their shoulders supporting water jars.

"They blame the lumber industry for causing this drought by stripping the land of its cover," said Som-Marie. "Each time I return to this region it is dryer than before. When I was younger you never saw women going after water like this. It is very sad."

They came to a group of huts and stopped at the small open front village store. The surrounding thatch huts were all on stilts. The few people were not so friendly but stood around quietly, staring at this little group. There were some soft drinks sold but no ice. Som-Marie spotted some familiar fruit, which she referred to as Looktaan, the fruit of the sugar palm. It contained about half a cup of sweet liquid inside and so they bought a sack full, again to conserve water.

"Wonder if we lost our pursuers," mentioned Stony, "I haven't noticed any dust clouds moving in our direction."

"I don't believe they could follow us on these roads with automobiles," said Som-Marie.

"Man, I'm sweating like a whore in church," complained JJ, "oops, sorry, Som-Marie, I shouldn't talk like that around a lady. Let me rephrase that. I oughta say I'm sweating like a stuck pig."

"No offense, JJ, and me too."

JJ continued talking, apparently uncomfortable about his verbal slip; he changed the subject as they took advantage of the storefront shade.

"You know, one time on the road to Pattaya, I kept passing piles of some white grain-like stuff, I mean it was piled right on the roadside. Smelled like a chicken house my grandma had. At least we don't have to put up with anything like that today." He turned to Som-Marie, "Got any idea what that was? I mean that was one powerful, disgusting smell."

"You were probably traveling during the cassava harvest, JJ."

"So what is that?"

"Do you like tapioca, JJ?"

"Yeh. So?"

"Those odorous piles were what they make tapioca from, among other things. It is called cassava or manioc."

"Whew! Maybe I oughta say I *used* to like tapioca."

There were several older women sitting on a straw mat, ignoring the visitors and conversing among themselves. Stony was observing them and several small children, who returned his smile.

"Som-Marie, these kids are cute, but these people aren't Thai, are they?"

"They are Karens. As I mentioned before, they have come out of Burma. And the red stained chins of those old women you were watching results from their chewing the betel nut, a mild narcotic."

"Fascinating," said JJ, "Must be a hard life around here. They seem to go from children to weathered old folks, with nothing in between."

"Almost, but not quite, JJ. Most of the young adults have gone off to the city to find work and send money home."

JJ shook his head, "Still a tough life. Well, all aboard."

They continued their slow westward trek down the rough, hot, dusty, trails. Finally, Som-Marie pointed to a narrow road to the right. JJ slowed and followed her directions.

They came to another small group of huts on stilts. A few pigs and a skinny dog were meandering about. Three small children were playing under one of the huts. JJ pulled up to the nearest one. Som-Marie got out and said something in a foreign tongue. No Response. She repeated it louder. A grizzled, toothless old woman pushed the thatch covering from a window and leaned out. After a little animated conversation, Som-Marie returned to the Jeep.

"If I understood her correctly, she said a foreigner and two Thais were living in a rented hut about three kilometers north of here. That would be near the shrine and water caves."

Stony grinned, "Let's hear it for the gossip grape-vine." He asked Som-Marie to repeat her description of the caves.

"As I said before, there are only two caves we should be interested in. The people we are after probably aren't from around here, and so shouldn't know about the many other caves. The cave most visited by people from out of the area has a large statue of the reclining Buddha. The cave is long and narrow, but because it has more than one opening the air circulates and it is relatively cool, and has many stalagmites. It also has electric lighting."

"By the way, Som-Marie," mentioned JJ, "how come there are so many statues of Buddha in various positions? When we put up a statue of somebody at home they are either just standing or sitting."

"There is a reason for that, JJ. In Buddhist's texts, hundreds of years old, each position is strictly spelled out, including the position of the hands and explaining the meaning of it all. For instance, in the cave here, the reclining Buddha represents the Buddha's dying moments when he reached for the ultimate stage of nirvana."

"You know," said Stony as they bounced along the rutted road, "I had wondered about that. Figured there was some religious significance about the details of those statues. What can you tell us about the other cave?"

"I haven't been there since I was a child and I remember it as a very scary place. It has one, huge, hot cavern. The local villagers go there to draw water. There is one water hole near the entrance, but the larger, better one is in the rear. That is why we went there, we were out of water. It took us at least half an hour to reach the rear of the cave. There are some dark, scary alcoves back there. We used flashlights, but the villagers use torches and so the walls are all smoked up and smelly. The floor is slimy and slippery, so you have to walk slowly. Oh, and there are hundreds of bats and huge, blind cave spiders everywhere." She pulled her arms up to her chest and shuddered at the memory.

A little further down the road, out of sight of the villagers, Stony opened the canvas bag and loaded the Defender shotguns with buckshot, propping one on each side of him. They drove to the entrance of the shrine cave and spoke to the caretaker. Yes, there were two Bangkok people renting a hut not far to the east of the cave. He hadn't seen any foreigners though.

They parked the Jeep just out of sight of the selected hut and carefully approached as close as they dared, using what they could for cover. The hut was in a wide clearing. There was no way to get up close in the daylight.

"Now what?" whispered JJ, "We just walk up to the door and ask if they'd like to buy some Girl Scout cookies?"

"It'll be dark in an hour and that ain't good. We'd better get something going real soon," said Stony.

"How about this?" said Som-Marie, "They don't know me. I can tell them I am lost from my pilgrimage group and ask for directions to the shrine cave. That way we can determine if anyone is in there and maybe get even more information."

"I don't know, sweetheart…" It was too late. She had stepped into the open and started forward. They readied themselves for trouble. It wasn't long in coming.

Som-Marie took only about a dozen steps when a single shot rang out from a thatch covered window. Her head snapped back and she crumbled to the ground.

Stony and JJ immediately opened fire on the window. Stony emptied his Defender, dropped it and dashed to Som-Marie. Blood flowed down the right side of her face. He scooped her up and ran for cover, not stopping until he reached the Jeep. Despite his efforts to remain calm, he was a bundle of emotion as he laid her gently across the back seat. Terrified that he may be losing her and in a rage against whoever had done this. He grabbed the first aid kit and a water bottle. Quickly but gently he cleaned the wound to determine its extent. He swabbed the blood from her face, thankful that she was at least still breathing. With great relief he realized that the bullet had only grazed her temple, deeply cutting but not penetrating. He stopped the bleeding and applied a head wrap bandage.

She would have a hell of a headache, but she would live. He made her as comfortable as he could, stepped from the Jeep and looked up into the sky, "Thanks Boss. I owe you one for this. I really owe you one." He raced back to JJ, who had moved.

"Over here," JJ yelled, "kept my eye on them. Two ran out the back of the hut and towards what looks like a cave out a ways. If there's any more, they must still be in the hut."

Stony recovered his Defender and reloaded, "Cover me." Full of rage, he raced to the hut, jumped to the porch and crashed full-body through the shut front door, ready to blast at anything that moved. Nothing moved.

"JJ!"

JJ ran forward, bounding up the flimsy steps and into the one room hut. On the floor was what was left of a young Thai woman. The shotguns had torn large holes in the thatch and made the girl otherwise unrecognizable.

"Means there was only three of them in here and one of the two running out back could've been Allan. Probably going to make a hostage out of him. I hate to even ask this Stony. How's Som-Marie? Is she…alive?"

"She's alive. Fortunately it was just a deep flesh wound to her right temple. She'll hurt plenty, but she's alive."

"Stony, when that shot was fired; I could've sworn I heard what sounded like Allan screaming, NO!"

They jumped from the hut and cautiously made their way towards the cave entrance. The vegetation was sparse, the trees stunted and dust covered, the ground powder dry.

"This sure ain't what most people would think of as Thailand," whispered JJ.

"Looks more like a war zone, doesn't it?"

Just then, two native women came running from the cave entrance, without water jars or torches. They ran a short distance, glancing back nervously. Stony and JJ watched as they encountered two other women carrying water jars approaching and animatedly warned them away, joining their retreat.

"Looks like the cave has been commandeered by the bad guys," said Stony. They crept to the right side of the entrance.

"JJ, do me a favor. Stay here and guard this entrance. I don't want innocent villagers shot, and I don't want to be ambushed by any more of this gang, if there are more. I know you are in charge, but I want to do this."

"I understand." He put his hand on Stony's shoulder and squeezed.

He handed his shotgun to JJ. He didn't know what he might encounter and wanted both hands free. Also, if there was a shoot-out in the dark, a shotgun pattern might get Allan too. With his pistol he could aim at the other guy's muzzle flare, and being an excellent shot, he could restrict his hit to an area close around it. Crouching, he entered the cave, passing through a short tunnel about six feet high and maybe twenty feet long, slanting to the right slightly. This was both good and bad. Good because it enabled him to get into the main cavern undetected, bad because any light from outside was quickly lost.

About forty feet in the floor began to get slippery, just as Som-Marie had said. He decided to follow the wall with one hand in order to have some semblance of direction. Without it in the pitch blackness he could quickly lose his bearings. He crept quietly along wondering where his enemy was. He heard a noise, barely, like metal hitting a rock. It wasn't loud and he couldn't be sure of where it was but it wasn't close. He kept inching forward. The noise maker had disturbed some bats. He could hear them flying about, some close to him. A large, blind, cave spider ran down his arm. He shook it off. He felt another drop on his head, one on his back. He had never liked spiders and this was disgusting. He kept knocking them off. He wished he could see something. Anything. It seemed he had been inching along for hours, although it was probably no more than twenty minutes. Should be coming near to the rear of the cave by now.

His fingers left the wall. As he turned to find it again, slightly off balance, his feet slipped and he fell. Pain exploded through his wounded side. The noise alerted the kidnapper who fired a shot in his direction. The sound was deafening in the rock cavern. He saw the muzzle flare and a spark as the bullet ricocheted off the ceiling above him. Not even close – but it told him his target was jumpy. Now he had a location, unless they moved.

Stifling a groan, he slowly and painfully made it to his feet and fished around in the dark to relocate the wall of the cave. He had passed an outcropping and missed the corner. Now his whole backside was wet and slimy like the floor. Since his fall had given the kidnapper his general location, and he had theirs, he decided on a little flanking maneuver.

Gritting his teeth to suppress any involuntary moans and putting his left hand out in front of him, and wondering why- the black emptiness seemed endless, he began slowly, quietly, walking at a right angle to the wall. He hoped to cross the cavern and move toward them from the opposite side. Carefully he placed each step at the proper angle to insure his direction. Absently, he began counting his steps…ninety, ninety-one… He put his foot down but there was nothing there. As he pulled back too quickly on this slimy, unforgiving floor, he lost his balance again. He hit hard on his butt, pain shot throughout his body, his weight carried him forward and suddenly there was nothing beneath him!

The back of his head hit the edge of the cave floor, momentarily stunning him. With a loud splash, he hit the water.

Groggily, he began to tread water, his survival instincts temporarily sustaining him. He shook his head, trying to chase the cobwebs. Now what the hell was he going to do? He didn't know which was stronger, the pain or the anger. Things were sure going to hell in a hurry. In a pitch black pool of water, no idea of direction, deprived of his primary sensory perception. The splash undoubtedly echoed throughout the cavern, unmistakably marking his location.

Was this going to be it? Would he see a flashlight beam up above followed by a shot? Now he knew what that old saying 'shooting fish in a barrel' felt like. He would be an easy target.

He had evidently found the water hole in the rear that Som-Marie had mentioned. The water was cool, not cold, and too deep to stand in. He began treading as silently as he could and moving forward. Any direction was better than none. The earlier loss of blood, the rough ride, and hitting his head as he fell into the water combined and he felt very weak and dizzy. Something hit his leg. Then again, he hoped whatever he was sharing the water with didn't bite. He tried to focus on more important things, like finding a way out.

He came to a wall and felt around, couldn't reach the top. It wasn't as slimy as the rest of the cave, but was too vertical and smooth to climb. He swam silently along it, checking out every inch, hoping for a handhold. Nothing. The wall dished to his right somewhat. He sensed a corner and a change of direction. He continued to follow the wall quietly. Surely the locals had fashioned a way out if someone were to fall in. He concluded it must have been a blind cave fish hitting him. He could handle that. Another corner. Inching along, constantly scanning the wall with his left hand as he treaded with his right. He was hurt and sore but survival urges kept him moving. A third shallow corner, if these were right angles, and he figured they were, one more and he would be back close to where he started. He didn't want to think about that.

There! A chip in the wall. He felt below and above, there were more. Small, chipped grooves. He could barely make use of them, they were so small. Quietly as he could mange, he began to climb; the water dripping off him seemed so loud. He slipped a couple of times, but didn't lose his grip. Slowly, with painful effort, especially from his injured side, he made his way upward. Finally, he could feel the cave floor. He slid over the edge and laid on the slimy surface, thankful to be there.

A flashlight beam began searching around him. Nowhere to hide. It settled on him and seemed incredibly bright for just a flashlight. He was temporarily blinded; even squinting he could see nothing but the small orb of light.

Then he heard it. The chilling sound of an automatic pistol slamming home the round. He summoned his pride and slowly rose to face his executioner.

The cavern erupted in light. He turned to see several large lights behind him.

"NOOOOO.......!"

The first flashlight holder fired, but not at him. Stony hit the deck. Suddenly the cave erupted in ear-shattering roars as the lights behind him opened fire on the shooter. There were two of them, now visible, and as he watched they staggered under the hits they were receiving. And then they were down.

The firing stopped but he continued to hug the slimy floor. The lights were moving towards him. Turning over, face up, he raised his hands in the air. Whoever these people were, rescuers or not, he would be no match for them.

Someone was approaching, too fast for the slippery floor. He braced for impact and sure enough the figure slipped and came sliding into his legs.

She grabbed him.

"Stony, are you all right? Ugh! You're soaking wet."

"Stopped for a refreshing swim, ma'am. Who's with you?"

"Captain Pibul, Mister McGraw," said a figure above him, the blinding lights preventing Stony from focusing. He could make out an outstretched hand and used it to get to his feet.

"Thanks, Captain. Now let's go see the results of your handiwork."

With the aid of Captain Pibul and Som-Marie, he made his way over to the pair. Just as he suspected, one of the victims of the shoot-out was Allan. He knelt down, felt for a pulse. Faint, but there.

"Allan! Allan! Can you hear me? It's Stony."

Slowly the eyes opened halfway, then squinting. The police moved their flashlights out of his face, while still lighting the area.

"Stony?... That you?" he coughed, eyes glazed.

"It's me, Allan," he said, picking him up slightly and cradling his head on the body of the 'kidnapper,' who happened to be the same kitoy they had seen him with that night in Patpong. It was obvious he wouldn't live long. There were too many wounds. Even with immediate medical attention he had no real chance and here in this remote cave, there was nothing anyone could do.

"Stony...gotta...tell you...something. I wasn't kidnapped...ran away...that message from...Richard...is he here?" He was struggling for breath, coughing, gurgling.

"Came and went Allan."

"Thought... he was...coming to...fire me. Ran away. Kidnapping...just a...ruse...buying time. Been a helluva...couple of days. Great sex...what a way to go, eh? So tired...Didi...that's what...he...she liked to be called. Insatiable...great sex. Wouldn't do it... with a guy, you know. Didi was...a man...but more like...a woman with a wanger...you know...insatiable...the whore and I so exhausted...sometimes...we'd just lay there...and let Didi use us..."

"I don't think we need to hear about that, Allan."

Allan slumped. Stony felt for a pulse. Allan opened his eyes again.

"Stony, your wife..." Stony leaned close; Allan's voice was almost a whisper now as he struggled to speak.

"What Allan. What about my wife? Do you know something?" Stony had hold of Allan's shoulders now, ignoring his own pain, picking him up off the floor.

"Know who…killed her." He was coughing, gasping.

"Who Allan? Who?" he was shouting.

"I did…she found out…about Didi…used same beauty parlor…she knew, Stony…was going to tell you. I didn't have…choice. Sorry, Stony, so sorry. "Would've ruined me…lost clearance, job…everything. I begged her…give me twenty-four hours…then I would…tell you. Thought bomb would fool you…it did." He smiled wanly, coughed. "But couldn't get you…go home. Didi put…some hits on you…I didn't know…until yesterday…honest…" he slumped again.

Stony looked up at Som-Marie and Captain Pibul through tear-filled eyes. JJ leaned down, put his fingers on Allan's neck.

"He's gone folks." He helped Stony to his feet, accepted a flashlight from one of the policemen and handed it to Som-Marie, who took Stony's arm and together they made their way slowly along the wall of the cave into the hot Thai night. Stony plodded along zombie-like until they reached the Jeep. It was finally over. The crushing weight of the past year, the frustrations, the disappointments, and the overwhelming sorrow, all came to the fore in an irresistible wave, one last time.

He climbed into the driver's seat, crossed his arms over the steering wheel and burying his head in them, he wept.

After a while, JJ approached and put his hand on Stony's shoulder.

"Wanna drive, 'ol buddy?"

Stony lifted his head, nodded negatively and climbed into the back with Som-Marie. The long return trip to Bangkok was made in silence. A little after midnight, JJ pulled up to the ambassador's guest house.

"We'll talk tomorrow. Call me when you're ready. I'd check that wound in your side, Stony, all that muck could cause an infection. You too, Som-Marie, that was a nasty blow. Want me to take you two to the hospital?" They declined.

After a long, hot shower they carefully cleaned and redressed each other's wounds and slumped into bed. They lay there awhile, holding each other, but Stony was lost in a world of his own.

He awoke to a familiar smell. Som-Marie poked her head in the door smiling, "Good afternoon, sir. Lunch is being served."

When he got to the table, Som-Marie was beaming, "The ambassador's kitchen is remarkably well stocked. The servants tell me they serve Mexican meals on occasion, by his request, but they had never made these. I had to call JJ for the recipe and we hope he remembered it correctly. I thought you might need a lift this morning." She raised the shiny metal domes off their plates.

"Mexican ranch eggs. Sorry, I can't say it in Spanish."

He hugged her, kissed her on the unwounded side of her forehead, "Huevos, my dear, huevos rancheros. How could a guy not be in love with a gal like you? This is real sweet."

"It's getting cold." She sat down, "I thought since you have been so good about eating our local cuisine, maybe I should try one of your favorite dishes." She took a few bites. "This is really delicious!"

"OK, JJ. The gang's all here. Let's have it," said Pete who put a paper cup in front of each of them as they each took a chair around the now familiar conference table. John was coming along behind him filling each cup.

JJ stood and said, "Alright. Stony, if I miss anything, just jump in anytime." Stony nodded.

"Alright folks, this is the way it was. Our Allan meets this kitoy, digs the sex; by the way, he claimed it was more like being with a woman than a man. Anyway, this kitoy happens to use the same hairdresser as Stony's wife. I guess in beauty parlors they talk about everything so she puts two and two together. Next time Allan shows up at their house, she asks him about it. She tells him that since she has never kept anything from her husband, she will have to tell him. Allan panics. As we all know, Allan's first reaction to any crisis is to panic, anyway he figures exposure will ruin him.

As you know, even though the Agency frowns on homosexuality; the real issue is if someone puts themselves in a position to be blackmailed and thus liable to give away classified information.

So, Allan begs for time to prepare himself to tell Stony. Instead, with time running out, he concocts a plan and manages to put a bomb in Stony's car, knowing that his wife will go to the hairdresser before going out that night. On a pretense, he picks Stony up for work that morning so the wife will use the car and not a taxi. He figures everybody will believe it was meant for Stony. He also figured Stony would accompany the children home. When 'ol Stony here managed to stay in Bangkok, Allan somewhat stonewalled the local investigation, afraid he would be found out." JJ was pacing the room, circling the table. He stopped and patted Som-Marie on the shoulder before continuing.

"Eventually, his lover, that kitoy, evidently to protect Allan's interest, starts putting out contracts on Stony. When these didn't work out, he told the local police that he had an eye-witness against Stony in the murder of his wife. When Allan read the message about Richard's arrival, right after I had sent those drinks in that bar, he again panics, sets up a fake kidnapping and skips town.

By the time Stony, Som-Marie and I track them down, they had picked up some whore-friend of the kitoy's and had been having a non-stop orgy in a rented thatched hut down south about a dozen miles from the Burmese border. When super-girl here decides to flush them out, the whore shoots her. Me and Stony take out the whore so the kitoy and Allan split for this water cave. Stony goes in after them," he grins at Stony, "He takes a little swim, while I guard the entrance, since we don't know if there may be others. I heard a shot, then nothing. Captain Pibul of Bangkok's finest shows up. They had followed us from Bangkok but we had lost them. After stopping off at a local army base for a deuce and a half truck, they tracked us down again. Good thing. I figure I got no choice but to let them in on what's happening. We all go in, including a patched-up Som-Marie, just in time to see the kitoy about to shoot Stony. Our little lady screams. The cops open fire. Unfortunately, they put a bunch of holes into Allan as well.

Before Allan dies, he confesses to everything, in front of Captain Pibul, and Stony is cleared. The cops brought back the three corpses in body bags. I will arrange for Allan's body to be shipped back to D.C. Sealed casket." He sat down, took a drink from his cup, "That's about it folks. Except for this," he reached into his back pocket and produced an envelope, "your long awaited ticket home, 'ol buddy."

Stony glanced at Som-Marie, then at JJ. He took the envelope, opened it, and extracted the ticket.

"JJ, this is for a flight two weeks from now."

"Yea. Might just be enough time for you two to heal up and finish an interrupted vacation."

EPILOGUE

Stony had barely set foot on American soil when the Tet Offensive of 31 January 1968 drastically changed the scale of the Vietnam War. Within eighteen months the Imperial hotel burned to the ground, killing twenty-one American guests. JJ was promoted from acting to permanent Chief of Station. Som-Marie spent the summer at Stony's ranch in Colorado and…well, that's another story.

The author, F.A. Rawe, (Tony to his friends) has always taken the road less traveled. Born and raised in Kentucky, he joined the Army at seventeen where he worked for three different U.S. Intelligence agencies. During this time he lived in Japan, Turkey, Switzerland, Austria and Bangkok where this novel, Thai Watch, is set.

After the military he combined his love of the outdoors and "old west" becoming a Colorado cattleman settling on a ranch in the high plains. Both careers have been filled with adventure lending firsthand experience with being shot, stabbed, set afire, re-arranged facial features, concussions and having both legs broken by an enraged bull. He half jokingly says his biography, if he ever writes one, would be titled after the road sign, "rough road ahead."

His next novel is set in Turkey.